Alena's brother turned back to him. "I am prepared to withdraw from the contest between us for the contract," he told Kiryl, "but only if instead of giving up Alena, you marry her."

Alena made a small, agonized sound of protest and denial. This could not be happening.

"No. You can't mean it, Vasilii. I won't marry him," Alena burst out passionately, with all the horror she felt at what she had heard clear in her voice. She continued before either of them could say anything. "I heard everything, Vasilii." She was deliberately keeping her back to Kiryl, unable to endure the thought of looking at him. "All of it—every single word."

From somewhere, she managed to drag up out of her pain a lifeline of anger for her to cling on to.

"You might think now that you have succeeded in your plan to use me to blackmail Vasilii into letting you win the contract, but you haven't," she told him fiercely. "And as for marrying you—I'd rather stay single all my life."

USA TODAY bestselling author

Penny Jordan

brings you

RUSSIAN RIVALS

Demidov vs. *Androvonov—let the most merciless of men win...*

Kiryl Androvonov
The Russian oligarch has one rival:
billionaire Vasilii Demidov. Luckily,
Vasilii has an Achilles' heel—his younger,
overprotected, beautiful half sister Alena....

Vasilii Demidov
After losing his sister to his bitter rival,
Vasilii is far too cynical to ever trust a woman. He
keeps a *very* close eye on his new secretary, Laura.
Best friends with Alena since childhood, Laura has
always had a crush on Vasilii,
but never expected to find herself at the
ruthless Russian's mercy....

The rivalry begins in...

THE MOST COVETED PRIZE—November
And concludes with
POWER OF VASILII—December

Only from Harlequin Presents®.

Penny Jordan

THE MOST COVETED PRIZE

RUSSIAN RIVALS

TORONTO   NEW YORK   LONDON
AMSTERDAM   PARIS   SYDNEY   HAMBURG
STOCKHOLM   ATHENS   TOKYO   MILAN   MADRID
PRAGUE   WARSAW   BUDAPEST   AUCKLAND

Recycling programs
for this product may
not exist in your area.

ISBN-13: 978-0-373-23787-6

THE MOST COVETED PRIZE

First North American Publication 2011

All about the author...
Penny Jordan

PENNY JORDAN has been writing for more than twenty-five years and has an outstanding record—more than 165 novels published, including the phenomenally successful *A Perfect Family; To Love, Honour and Betray, The Perfect Sinner;* and *Power Play,* which hit the *Sunday Times* and *New York Times* bestseller lists. She says she hopes to go on writing until she has passed the 200 mark, and maybe even the 250 mark.

Although Penny was born in Preston, Lancashire, U.K., where she spent her childhood, she moved to Cheshire as a teenager, and has continued to live there. Following the death of her husband, she moved to the small traditional Cheshire market town on which she based her Crighton books.

She lives with her Birman cat, Posh, who tries to assist with her writing by sitting on the newspapers and magazines Penny reads to provide her with ideas she can adapt for her fictional books.

Penny is a member and supporter of the Romantic Novelists' Association and the Romance Writers of America—two organizations dedicated to providing support for both published and yet-to-be-published authors.

Books by Penny Jordan

Harlequin Presents®

2969—GISELLE'S CHOICE*
2999—A STORMY SPANISH SUMMER

*The Parenti Dynasty

CHAPTER ONE

ALENA had known she wanted him—quite desperately—the minute she'd seen him. That had been in the foyer of this London hotel earlier in the week. The fierce surge of previously unknown and unexpected sheer physical desire that had struck had been so powerful that it had almost literally knocked her off her feet—and left her in no doubt as to its meaning or its urgency, shaking tremulously from head to foot and on fire with the force of her own desire.

He was, she suspected, everything that her elder half-brother Vasilii had so often warned her against in his own sex. He was dangerous; she knew that—any woman would know it, even if Vasilii tried to treat her as though she was still merely a girl and not a woman.

Alena sighed. She did genuinely and really

love Vasilii, even if he was the most aggravat-
ingly old-fashioned, moralistic and over-pro-
tective brother anyone could have. However,
there was something about *him* which drew
and compelled her beyond reason, beyond
duty, beyond anything and everything she
had ever known or expected to know. Had
she been struck by love? Had she been struck
by its darker sibling lust? Or perhaps a combination of both? Was it her passionate deep-
running Russian blood that was responsible?
Or was it a vulnerability to wickedly dangerous Russian men she had inherited from her
English mother, who had fallen so swiftly in
love with her own Russian father?

It didn't matter. What was happening to her
was beyond the skills of analysis drilled in
to her to fit its pupils for the modern age by
the teachers at her all female and very strict
school. Nothing mattered other than the gath-
ering, growing rushing need that now owned
her. His air of openly raw sexuality and her
need to offer herself up to it, to be consumed
by it, filled her senses, leaving no room for
anything else. Just the thought of even breathing the same air as him was enough to send

her dizzy with delight and to make her body react as erotically as though he was already touching it, caressing it, taking it and touching it, teaching it and her everything that it meant to be a woman.

Alena shuddered in mute acknowledgement of his mastery of her responses. Any minute now he would turn and see her, and recognise the effect he was having on her. Her heart gave a fierce bound of mingled anticipation and apprehension. Oh, yes, he was dangerous—and she ached for it, hungered for it, craved it.

She might 'only' be nineteen, as Vasilii was so fond of reminding her, but she was more than old enough to know from the one tremulous, daring glance she had risked earlier in the week into those malachite-green eyes—so matching in colour the awesome columns of malachite in St Petersburg's Winter Palace—exactly what the man now standing engaged in conversation with another Russian on the other side of the exclusive hotel's even more exclusive lounge lobby was. He was living, breathing, walking sexual danger—especially to a woman like her. He lived outside convention and its rules.

Her pulse beating increasingly speedily, she studied him covertly and eagerly. He was tall—as tall as Vasilii, who was six feet three to her own five feet nine. He was also slightly younger than Vasilii, she suspected. Perhaps in his early thirties, whereas Vasilii was now thirty-five. His thick hair was a rich tawny brown, reminding her of the colour of one of Vasilii's hunting jackets, although this man's hair was in need of a cut to bring it to the kind of order Vasilii favoured.

Everywhere in his face—its bone structure, its contours, its expression—there were subtle traces of a heritage that said that this man came from a long line of men born to battle against other members of his own sex and to stand over their prone bodies when he had defeated them. He was pure alpha male, and a man determined to challenge anyone who questioned his right to that heritage.

His name was Kiryl Androvonov. She savoured it inside her head, unrolling it like a glittering magnificent carpet of delights for her senses. She had felt so adult, so strong and in control of her own fate, when she had asked the doorman so studiedly, mock-casually, if he knew who he was, pretending that she had recognised him as an acquaintance of her brother. The name Kiryl meant 'noble', but the doorman had told her only that he was a businessman and that this was his second visit to the hotel.

Kiryl hadn't intended to look for her—the slender, gazelle-like young woman with her silky fall of dark blonde hair and her silver-grey eyes that reminded him of sunlight on the frozen Neva river in winter, or the Russian fables of the *rusilki*, the fatal enchantresses who rose from their watery graves to lure men to join them. For one thing she wasn't his type, and for another he had far more important things on his mind than accepting the unspoken but implicit invitation she was giving him.

But he *had* looked, and she *was* there, in the same chair, at the same table, pouring tea from the steaming traditional samovar that the hotel indulged its Russian guests by providing.

She wasn't wearing a wedding ring—not that that meant anything these days. A high-priced hooker, then, dangling her bait? Maybe, but Kiryl doubted it. A hooker would have moved in on him before now—time was, after all, money in any business.

She wanted him, though. He knew that. But he did not want her. Nor did he intend to allow himself to want her, even if that no doubt astronomically expensive soft silk top she was wearing *was* outlining the undeniably natural and highly desirable shape of her breasts with all the sensual mastery of a skilled artistic hand. The top, which covered her from her throat right down to her wrists, shouldn't have been sexy. Those impossibly small-for-male-fingers shimmering pearl buttons that closed the neckline all the way from her throat to her breastbone should not have filled him with a desire to wrest them from their closures and lay bare to his gaze and his touch the flesh that lay beneath them—but they did. The diamond stud earrings she was wearing—if real, and he suspected that they were—would have cost whoever had given them to her many thousands of pounds. He knew that because his last mistress had tried to inveigle him into buying her a similar pair, just before he had decided that she no longer interested him.

As he assessed them—and that was all

he was assessing—she looked up and right at him, the colour coming and going in her face, dark lashes sweeping down over the silver-grey eyes which had gone from shining like the frozen Neva to burning with the glow of heated mercury...or the desire of a very aroused woman. Unexpectedly his own body responded to that swift change from the winter ice of St Petersburg to the fierce summer heat of the Russian steppes, with all the passion that the land of his fathers always inspired in him, as fiercely as though she held within her the essence of all that heritage meant to him. He could feel within him the surge of his own desire to take and possess that heritage; to claim it and to refuse to yield it to anyone.

Caught off-guard by the surge of electric male arousal gripping him, Kiryl recognised that the woman, whoever she was, was causing his attention to wander from something far more important than some left-over youth fantasy about possessing a woman who would somehow be a magical link between himself and his Russian heritage, earthing him in his right to it.

'And, as I was saying, Vasilii Demidov will

be your main stumbling block to winning the contract.'

Kiryl stiffened and focused his attention on the agent he had hired to help him win the contract he was determined to have for his business. The knowledge that one of Russia's richest men was also a contender for the contract had not put him off. Far from it. It had merely sharpened his desire to win it.

'Demidov has not previously shown any interest in the shipping or container industry. His business interests lie mainly in owning and controlling the port side of the business,' Kiryl pointed out. 'Therefore he has no reason to have any interest in the contract.'

'He hadn't, but he is currently in China, finalising another contract, and as part of the bargain the Chinese want a controlling interest in a container shipping line. He is in a position to undercut any price you may offer, even if that means acquiring the contract at an initial loss. I have it on the very best authority that the selection process for the contract is now down to the two of you, with the dice loaded very heavily in his favour. I'm afraid that I must warn you that with Demidov as your competition you cannot win.'

Kiryl gave his agent a hard look.

'I refuse to accept that.'

He could not and would not lose this contract. It was the final building block, the final piece in the chess game of his business life, that would establish his supremacy in his chosen field—not just in his own eyes but in the eyes of Russia itself. No one could be allowed to stop him from achieving that goal. *No one.* He had worked too hard and too long to let that happen.

Inside his head an image formed: a man's profile, his eyes hard and denying, rejecting the child he had been. His father. The father who had denied him not just the right to his name but also the right to his Russian blood. Just as Vasilii Demidov would if he now denied him the right to complete the end game he had striven for so long.

'Then you must hope for a miracle—because that is what it will take for you to beat Demidov and win this contract.'

Typically Kiryl did not allow any of what he was feeling to show in his demeanour or his voice, simply saying, in a voice as relentlessly cold as winter, 'There must be something that would make him back off—some way of undermining him. A man does not make the money he has made without having secrets in his past he would not want exposed.'

The agent inclined his greying head in acknowledgement of Kiryl's statement before warning him, 'You are not the first man to look for some weakness in Demidov that can be exploited, but there isn't one. He is armour plated. He has no vulnerability, no known past sins to catch up with him, and no present vices to use against him. He is impregnable.'

Kiryl's mouth hardened.

'He is impressive, I agree. But no man is impregnable. There will be a way, a vulnerability—and I promise you this: I will find it, and I will use and exploit it.'

The agent remained silent. He knew better than to argue with the man facing him. Kiryl had grown to his wealth and his present position of authority and power through the hardest and most challenging of circumstances—and it showed.

Nevertheless, he felt obliged to remind him

as they parted, 'As I have already said, what you require if you are to win out against Demidov is a miracle. Take my advice and back out now—let him have the contract. That way at least you will save face and not have to endure the humiliation of publicly losing to him.'

Back out? When he was so close to fulfilling the vow he had made to himself so many years ago? *Never.*

Could she risk picking up her teacup now, without her hands trembling so much that she risked spilling the hot liquid? Alena wasn't sure. Her heart was still jumping around inside her chest cavity, and her face was still burning from the effect that one piercing brilliant green gaze had had on her. He had looked right at her. She put her hands on her still hot cheeks in an attempt to cool them down. She must not look at him again. She simply didn't have the strength to withstand the raw maleness of such a gaze. It had melted her insides, turning them into a soft liquid pulse of longing that quivered within her still. And yet she had to look—she had to let her senses and her body drink in their fill of the dangerous excitement of all that fierce sexual masculinity.

Her pulse had started to race, and her throat was so dry that she had to swallow hard as she allowed her head to turn again in his direction, the longing and excitement beating even more fiercely than ever inside her with anticipation—only to crash down to wretched disappointment when she realised that he wasn't there. He had gone, and thanks to her silly, immature stupidity she had missed her chance to…to what? To prolong the intensity of that mesmerising gaze until her bones melted and her heart burst with the unbearable excitement of it? He might have come over, introduced himself. He might have…

There was something on the floor—a gold pen. It must be his. He must have dropped it. Quickly Alena rose from her seat and went to pick it up. It felt cool and hard against her fingertips. She was shaking so much that she couldn't stand up again without her head swimming. She could see him standing close to the hotel exit. The man he had been with was leaving the hotel. Was he going to follow him? Without allowing herself the chance to think about what she was doing, Alena crossed the hotel foyer.

The click of her heels alerted Kiryl to her presence. When she walked she swayed as delicately as the silver birches in Russia's northern forests.

'You dropped this.'

Her voice was as soft as the sigh of a spring breeze, cooling the stuffy, over-heated hotel air as it brushed his skin.

She was holding out a pen to him. Not his pen, but he took it from her nonetheless. Her hand was delicately boned, her fingers long and slim, her nails buffed to a natural sheen. She had a look about her that money alone could not buy: a translucent, shimmering natural beauty allied to the kind of discreet grooming that whispered privilege and protection. This woman had been feather-bedded from the moment of her birth.

Angry with himself for being so aware of her, he punished her for that awareness by telling her mockingly, 'And of course you would seize such a golden opportunity to return it to me, wouldn't you? Given your interest in me. Hasn't anyone ever told you that it is the male's role to pursue his quarry and reveal his desire, not the female's.'

Hot colour ran up under Alena's skin like burning fire. She deserved his mockery—and his cruelty: Vasilii would have said so. But she hadn't been prepared for it and it hurt. Inside her head—foolishly—she had built up an image of him in which his danger was tempered by a desire for her that matched her own for him. Now she was being made to pay for that fantasy.

Kiryl watched as she struggled to overcome her humiliation, pride battling against pain as her small white teeth bit so hard into that soft bottom lip that it swelled swiftly. Just as it would swell beneath the fierce demand of a man's kiss? Against his will Kiryl felt the ache in his groin the sight of her had aroused earlier return—with interest.

'My apologies. That was ungracious of me.'

His apology was deliberately insincere. He didn't have either the time or the desire to deal with the fragile ego of an emotional woman—no matter how desirable. He knew himself too well, and he knew that in the mood he was in now, thanks to Vasilii Demidov, the darkness within him that he had never wholly been able to control would unleash itself and seek a victim. Over the years Kiryl had taught himself to think of that darkness as something of a mental vampire, an echo of himself that, when aroused, could only be calmed by feeding off the emotional pain of others. No doubt there were those who would say that that dark need sprang from his childhood, but Kiryl had no intention of dwelling on a time when he had been vulnerable. Instead he preferred to live in the present, and living in the present meant securing that contract. The girl was simply a spare pawn in the game, and as such he had no use for her other than as a momentary outlet for his pent-up inner frustration with regard to his bid and the competition he was up against.

For Alena, though, his caustic cruelty was unbearable. She retreated from him, feeling too upset and too humiliated to defend herself, merely shaking her head and turning away to hurry back to her table.

Once there she asked for her bill and proceeded to gather up her coat and her bag. She had shown herself up most dreadfully. She deserved the punishment he had meted out, she told herself. She was just glad that her half-brother hadn't been there to witness it. Fresh tears blurred her vision.

Automatically Kiryl tracked her uncoordinated, anxiously urgent movements. Because he wanted to distance himself from her, that was all. And yet his gaze and his senses were somehow reluctant to let her go. Even now, when she was plainly upset, there was still a grace about her, a breathtaking natural sensuality, a pliable softness—from the top of her shining fall of dark blonde hair to the delicacy of ankles so fine Kiryl suspected he could easily close his hand around them—that said the whole of her could be bent to the will of the man who possessed her.

And did he want to be that man? It wasn't so much a matter of wanting as of taking advantage of what he was being offered so blatantly. Kiryl shrugged aside his inner criticism of himself. He was, after all, a man—with a man's needs. And it was obviously what *she* wanted. She had practically been begging for it, and it would be one way of ridding himself of the anger he felt at having his plans threatened by Vasilii Demidov. He had taken the savagery of the sharp raw edge off it via his mockery of her. He could make amends quite easily. He knew the format. She would initially pretend to refuse to allow him to do so. He would then flatter her and she would give in. It was a game as old as life itself, and an hour or so in bed with her in his suite would surely be enough to satisfy the ache in his groin.

A brief movement of his hand summoned a waitress. Giving her his instructions, he made his way over to the table.

Alena was just about to leave, her back to him as she waited for another waitress to bring her bill.

'You didn't drink your tea earlier, and since I am very much in need of a cup why don't we share a samovar together? Two Russians together, sharing a tradition from our home-land?'

The unexpected sound of his voice had Alena spinning round, her shock intensifying when he reached out and closed long fingers around her wrist, his thumb on her unsteady, far too fast pulse.

His smile was pure megawatt charm. It softened the earlier arrogant harshness of his features and turned him into every woman's fantasy of a bad boy grown into an adult male. It gave him the sensuality of a Cossack, the romance of a gypsy, the wild devilry of a pirate and the alpha allure of a hero. With that smile he was all of them and more. And she would be a fool to give in to him.

'No, thank you.' She tried to sound distant and cool, but she knew he had heard the vulnerable huskiness of her voice, the note of doubt and longing that undermined her will-power. Her throat felt dry and raw with emotion and tension. She wanted to wrench her wrist free of his hold but somehow she couldn't.

He was smiling at her again, more intimately this time, the malachite eyes darkening and gleaming.

'I was rude and I upset you, and now you are angry with me. You think, no doubt, that I do not deserve your company. And you are right. After all, such a beautiful woman can easily find a far more pleasant and appreciative companion. But I think you have a kind heart, and that that kind heart will whisper to you to take pity on me.'

Oh, yes, he could be very charming—as well as very cruel. And Alena didn't need Vasilii to tell her how dangerous that made him. Every woman carried within her DNA the instinctive knowledge of just how dangerous such a man could be. And just how compellingly and demandingly irresistible.

The smile that accompanied his apology revealed strong white teeth and crinkled the skin around his eyes. Its effect on her locked the breath in her lungs and started a stampede of small butterfly movements of shocked but exhilarating excitement fizzing in her stomach. The hurt he had already caused her had left its mark, though—like a bruise against pale vulnerable skin and her brain warned her to be careful.

He was massaging her skin, stroking that place where her pulse was thudding so tempestuously, but far from soothing her his touch was only increasing her agitation and her awareness of him. She must escape from him whilst she still could. He was dangerous, and she was not equipped to deal with that danger.

'I must go. I…'

Her English was refined and unaccented.

Despite the samovar he had seen on the table she did not look or sound Russian, except for those silver-grey eyes that reminded him so intensely of the Neva and the city of his birth. And the pain he had known there...

'I have ordered our tea. See—the waitress is bringing it now.'

Two waitresses were heading for the table— one carrying fresh tea, the other bringing her bill. The waitress with her bill smiled at her and said politely, 'I am sorry, Miss Demidova. I thought you wanted your bill.'

She *was* Russian. She had to be with that surname. And not just any Russian surname either. The irony of her sharing the same surname—a relatively common one in Russia—as his rival for the contract he wanted so badly was not lost on Kiryl. Perhaps it was an omen. The voluntary foster mother or *babushka*, who had raised him after the death of his own mother, along with several other orphaned and unwanted children, had set great store by old superstitions and beliefs, but he did not. He was a modern man, after all.

'You're staying here in the hotel?' he asked, pulling out a chair for Alena with his free hand

and firmly guiding her into it, leaving her no option other than to remain at the table.

He was even more magnificent, more imposing, more heart-stoppingly male close up than he had been at a distance. In the rarefied heated air of the hotel he somehow managed to smell of the clean air of the Russian steppes, with an underlying note of their wildness that brought the tiny hairs up along her skin. Oh, yes—he was dangerous.

'Yes.' She answered his question. 'My brother Vasilii has a concierge apartment here in the hotel for when he's in London on business.' Her half-brother was something of a nomad, and although he had similar apartments all over the world, and his most permanent address was an apartment in Zurich, there was nowhere that he really called home.

Alena wasn't quite sure if she was so pointedly introducing her brother into the conversation to warn Kiryl that she was not unprotected and alone, or to remind herself how Vasilii would judge her *own* behaviour were he to learn of it. Vasilii, who thought she was safely in the care of the now retired matron of the girls' school Alena had attended, whom he had hired to stay with her whilst she was away. Poor Miss Carlisle, though, had been rushed into hospital with appendicitis, and was now recovering from an operation in the comfortable nursing home where Alena had insisted she go to to recuperate.

Her absence was giving Alena a brief period of unexpected freedom, but Alena did feel guilty about the way she had deceived Miss Carlisle by letting her think that the niece she had begged Alena to contact on her behalf was now standing in for her. It wasn't her fault that Miss Carlisle's niece had left for New York the day before Miss Carlisle had fallen ill. She should have told Vasilii what had happened, of course, but she hadn't. Her brother was still under the illusion that Miss Carlisle, who flatly refused to have anything to do with modern technology and thus would not use a computer or a mobile telephone, was staying in the apartment with Alena to look after her.

Kiryl's heart had jerked to a standstill, almost cutting off his breath and leaving him feeling almost as though he was at a hangman's mercy. Surely it was beyond coincidence that there could be two Vasilii Demidovs—both of whom were wealthy enough to maintain a suite in one of London's most expensive hotels? Perhaps there had after all been some grain of truth in his old *babushka's* superstitious beliefs about the workings of fate?

Kiryl, though, had not built up his business and his own status as a billionaire by making assumptions that were not based on properly sourced fact.

After waiting for the waitress to pour their tea and then withdraw, he asked casually, 'Your brother is Vasilii Demidov? Head of Venturanova International?'

'Yes,' Alena confirmed, a small frown puckering her forehead as she asked anxiously, 'Do you know Vasilii?'

Was she concerned—anxious—about the possibility of him knowing her brother? Like all hunters Kiryl had a good nose for vulnerability in his prey.

'Not personally. Although naturally I do know of him and his reputation as a successful businessman. Is he here in London?' Kiryl knew that he wasn't, but he wanted to know how much the girl would tell him.

'No. He's in China. On business.'

'Leaving you, his sister, to amuse herself here in London, enjoying its nightlife?' he suggested with another smile.

Immediately Alena shook her head. 'Oh, no. Vasilii would never allow me to do that. He doesn't approve of that kind of thing—especially for me,' she admitted, immediately flushing guiltily. She was saying far too much. Certainly saying and doing things that Vasilii would most definitely not have approved of, because she felt so nervous and so excited.

'He sounds a very protective brother,' Kiryl told her. A very protective brother who believed in guarding something—someone—who was very important to him. He needed to find out more about her and her relationship with her brother.

'Yes he is.' Alena answered Kiryl's question, caught off guard. 'And sometime…'

'You find that irksome and inhibiting?' he guessed. 'You are young. It's only natural that you want to enjoy the same kind of life as other people. It must be lonely for you—left here on your own here in an anonymous hotel whilst your brother goes about his business.'

'Vasilii *is* very protective. He doesn't leave me on my own. At least not normally. This time, though… This time he had to.' Again Alena felt that pang of guilt she had every time she thought about how she was deceiving her brother. But, much as she liked Miss Carlisle, she was very old and very old-fashioned. Everything had been so different when their parents had been alive. Their father had been so energetic, so filled with an enjoyment of life, and her mother had been so loving, and so understanding. Alena missed them both dreadfully, but especially her mother.

Something was going on here. Kiryl's sharply keen senses told him that. Some undercurrent the meaning of which with regard to his own plans he had yet to divine and define.

He lifted one eyebrow and joked, 'He sounds more like a gaoler than a brother.'

Alena immediately felt guilty again. She was being horribly disloyal to Vasilii, but at the same time there was a sense of relief and release for her in talking about how she felt. Something about this intense stranger had her opening up about things she'd never confided to anyone before. Even so, her love for her brother insisted that she defend him and correct Kiryl's misconceptions.

'Vasilii is protective of me because he loves me, and because…because he promised our father when he was dying that he would always look after me.' She dipped her head. 'I worry sometimes that it is because of that promise that Vasilii has never married. Because of the business and because he worries so much about me that he has never had time to meet someone and fall in love.'

Fall in love? What planet was the girl living on if she actually thought that the marriage of one of Russia's richest men would involve 'falling in love'? Not that he blamed Demidov for that. When the time came for him to marry himself his wife would be carefully chosen, by a logical process, not by some temporary burn of desire in his loins. Not that he was going to tell Alena that. The more she revealed to him the more convinced he became that this young woman—this girl, really—just might be his rival's Achilles' heel.

Kiryl wasn't someone who gave in to his own emotions, though. Always back up gut instinct with hard facts before acting—that was his own personal mantra, and he wasn't going to go against that now, no matter how urgently the voice inside him was demanding that he now secure without delay his bait he might be able to use in a trap set against his rival for the contract.

Hard facts closed traps. A mixture of gut instinct backed up by hard facts was what he lived by.

Alena's emotional defence of her brother had warmed the silver-grey of her eyes. They were like deep clear pools within which he could see each and every one of her thoughts, Kiryl recognised, as she looked at him over the rim of her teacup and then flushed, quickly concealing her gaze with the dark fan of her eyelashes.

It had been wrong of her to discuss Vasilii with Kiryl. He was, after all, a stranger, and she knew how Vasilii felt both about protecting her and protecting his own privacy. She put down her teacup.

'I really must go.'

Kiryl nodded his head, and then got up.

'Thank you for the tea,' Alena told him as he summoned the waitress.

'It was my pleasure—and it was just the first of many pleasures I hope we shall enjoy together, Alena Demidova.'

Before Alena could guess his intent, he reached for her hand and lifted it to his mouth. Just the sensation of the warmth of his breath on her trembling fingers was enough to send hot molten quivers of sensation racing up her arm, making her feel weak with awareness of her vulnerability to him. He was flirting with her, and more than fulfilling the fantasies she had been indulging in ever since she had first seen him with the sensual promise implicit in his words.

As she moved she caught sight of her watch. Vasilii! There would be e-mails from him and he would worry if she did not reply speedily to them.

'It's four o'clock. I really must go. My brother...'

'Ah, like Cinderella fearing the stroke of midnight you rush to leave me—and without so much as a shoe to trace you by. But we shall meet again. Have no doubt about that. And

when we do I shall be tempted to ensure that
the promise I have seen in your eyes when you
look at me becomes more than just a look.'

CHAPTER TWO

IN THE privacy of his own suite Kiryl telephoned his agent, announcing the minute the older man answered the call, 'Alena Demidova, sister of Vasilii Demidov—I want to know everything there is to know about her.'

From the windows of his suite he could look out on the private garden in the square below, where the February light was now beginning to fade. A young East European woman was walking there with two children, both of them wearing the uniform of an exclusive prep school, but Kiryl had no interest in the garden or its occupants. All his intention was focused on the game plan now unfolding inside his head.

'Everything, Ivan—from who her friends are, how she spends her time, to what she eats for her breakfast. I want to know it all. And even more importantly I want to know everything there is to know about her relationship with her brother Vasilii, and his with her. I want to know what he thinks of her and what he plans for her. And I want to know by tomorrow morning.'

Ending the call before the other man could say anything, Kiryl paced the floor of the sitting room of his suite.

He could feel his whole body tingling with a potent mixture of excitement, challenge, and the knowledge that he had embarked on a game he would win. Alena was the key to her brother's downfall. He was sure of it. He could sense it, smell it, and feel it deep down inside himself in the Romany genes given to him by his mother and so loathed and despised by his father.

Unexpectedly inside his head he had a momentary image of Alena as she had been when they had had tea together—as fragile as a flower a man might pick and then crush in his hand, her emotions and desires plain to see. Something was struggling to come to life inside him—something that had its roots in that brief time he had shared with his mother before she had died, the only time in his life when he had been truly loved. For a moment he hesitated. But he could not afford to be weak—not now. As weak as the mother who had loved his father and conceived him against that father's wishes. He'd had to be strong in everything he had striven so long and hard for, goaded and driven during his struggle by the memory of the man who had been his father sneering down at him as he pushed him into the gutter before walking away from him.

It was finally within his grasp. And if Alena had to be sacrificed so that he could keep the mental promise he had made his dead mother, then so be it.

'The promise I have seen in your eyes when you look at me.' In the grey London light of the February morning Alena lay in the bed in her expensively designed and decorated bedroom, cocooned in the highest thread-count sheets that money could buy, but feeling every bit as uncomfortable as though she were that fairytale princess lying on the discomfort of a sharp pea. Fairytales. Wasn't that what this was all about? A young woman's fairytale, though, rather than a child's. A fairytale of a prince who wasn't just handsome and kind but a prince who was also sensual and sexy—a prince who offered not the experience of a pampered, indulged lifestyle, but the experience of real raw sensuality...the kind of intensely emotional and passionate sex that perhaps *was* merely a fantasy.

Was that why she now felt so unnerved and afraid? Because now that she had been given a hint that she could make her fantasy reality she feared that she might discover that being sexually involved with Kiryl would destroy that fantasy? Sex with Kiryl. Intimacy with Kiryl. The intimacy of shared kisses and caresses, her skin shivering with excitement, and the enticement of his hands—his lips—on her naked body. She was shivering with that excitement now, at the mere thought of it. But wasn't the reality that she needed to put him out of her thoughts and out of her life? That was certainly what Vasilii would want her to do.

Alena looked at her alarm clock.

She had an appointment later in the morning at the offices of a charity set up by her mother. Vasilii would prefer her to wait until she was twenty-five to step into her mother's shoes and fully take over her role at the head of the charity, Alena knew. He felt that even at twenty-one—which she would be in just over fifteen months—she would be still too young for such a responsibility. Alena, though, was determined to prove her half-brother wrong. She had been assiduous in studying the workings of the charity since her mother's death.

It *was* a big responsibility—a huge responsibility, in fact. The charity handled not only the income from the millions her parents had donated to it, but also the income that came from various sponsors and donors to the charity's cause, which was the education of children who would not otherwise receive any. How much chance would she have of convincing her half-brother that she was ready to take on that responsibility if he ever got to know of her reckless fantasies and even more reckless behaviour over Kiryl? None at all. He would judge such behaviour as immature and irresponsible.

Her mother had often said that the charity was her 'thank-you' to life for giving her the happiness that meeting her Russian husband had brought her. Not even Vasilii, with his often hard-headed attitude towards money and charity, could argue with that motivation. No matter how much she sometimes objected to Vasilii's control of her and her life, Alena knew full well that he had the power to melt her heart simply because he had loved and valued her mother so much. For such a tough, uncompromising man to be willing to admit that one slim Englishwoman had, through her love for his father and for him, transformed their lives—even if he would only admit that to her—was something that would always touch her heart. Vasilii's love and concern for her, his protection of her, was his way of repaying the love he had received from her mother, Alena knew. She just wished that he would relax his protective guard of her a little.

Did she really want to risk everything she had worked so hard for just for the sake of a sensual infatuation that had as much reality to it as a rainbow over the Neva?

She had no need to ask herself what Vasilii would think of her present behaviour. He would be horrified and angry. But he was not going to know about it, was he? Because she was going to be very sensible and responsible and not have anything more to do with Kiryl. She was going to focus instead on the future she had been working so hard towards and prove to her brother that she was mature enough to take on her late mother's role within the charity.

Two hours later, stepping out of her taxi outside the office block that housed the offices of her mother's charity, Alena paused to smooth down the soft grey cashmere of her smart single-breasted coat and take a deep breath. Appearances counted for an awful lot, her mother had always said. Deals could be brokered as broken in the judgement passed on the impression one conveyed—before a word had been spoken. Alena had remembered her mother's sage advice this morning when she had dressed for this appointment. It might eventually be her right and inheritance to take over the running of the charity, but she could not do that successfully without the support of the executives who worked for it. She needed to win their support and their confidence if she was going to be able to continue to grow the success of her mother's charity. For that reason she had tried to dress in a way that, whilst showing something of her own individuality, conveyed maturity.

She had chosen to wear medium-height black shoes with opaque winter tights rather than high-heeled knee-length boots. Boots might be sensible in cold weather, but there were boots and boots—and she certainly did not want to be judged as an attention-seeking fashion plate. To ward off the sharp February wind she'd wrapped a darker grey woollen scarf round her neck and pulled a matching knitted hat on over her hair. A pair of fingerless grey gloves allowed her to pay her taxi fare, and her smile for the doorman who opened the glass doors to the office block for her earned her an answering smile of appreciation.

Initially, when she'd first set up the charity, her mother had wanted to locate its head office in London because it was her home city. But she'd wanted it to be in a far more modest and inexpensive place than its current Mayfair location. It had been her father and half-brother who had persuaded her mother to accept that if the charity was to attract donors then a more prestigious location would give it gravitas. Besides which Vasilii had added a properly secured office block so it would be far safer.

Safety was important to Vasilii. But that was not surprising, given that his own mother had been the victim of a kidnap plot that had gone wrong, and which had resulted in her death. It had been after that that Vasilii's father had relocated his business and his home to London, although it had been in St Petersburg in Russia where her parents had met. Her father had had high moral standards, both in his business and his private life. The death of both parents in a car accident had been a terrible shock and a terrible loss, but thankfully she had always had Vasilii.

It had been wrong of her to allow herself to be taken over by what she was now beginning to think of as a form of madness in her unfamiliar desire for Kiryl, and she was glad that she had decided to put the whole incident behind her—to focus on what was really important in her life, Alena told herself as she stepped into the lift and pressed the button for the tenth floor.

The work of Alena's mother's charity involved helping girls in poverty all over the world. A multicultural staff worked for the charity, and its South American CEO, Dolores Alvarez, had known poverty in her childhood herself. She was now in her fifties, and the lines on her face told of her compassion and her life experience.

She welcomed Alena with a warm smile as she showed her into her office, and ordered coffee for both of them, telling her, 'We've had a lovely surprise this morning. You'll know that one of your late mother's goals for our charity was to bring in more outside donors, and that we've been running a campaign to that effect?'

Alena nodded her head. 'Yes, I know how important my father and mother believed it was that we should broaden the scope of the charity.'

'After the death of your parents we did receive some very generous donations from their colleagues and friends, but they were one off payments. However, we have now had an approach from a potential donor which sounds very promising. Before making up his mind he has stated that he wants to meet you.'

Their coffee had arrived, and after thanking the smartly dressed young male PA who had brought it Alena asked the CEO, 'Is it because he wants to know if I am capable of heading the charity successfully?' She gave Dolores a wry look and told her, 'It's exactly the kind of thing Vasilii would do.'

'Rich men like to be in complete control of their wealth. It seems to go with their mindset and the drive that has made them rich in the first place.'

'Control freaks?' Alena said ruefully.

Dolores smiled, but gave a small shake of her head. 'Maybe, but we can't afford to look a gift horse in the mouth, or…'

'Frighten it away?' Alena suggested.

'No. Not if we're to succeed in achieving the most ambitious of your late mother's plans. The money she left in trust for the charity brings in a good income, but…'

'But we need more money. Yes, I know. I've been studying our financial statements, and the rise in the cost of living in some of the countries where we are most active has meant that the cost of providing schooling for the poorest in those countries is rising.'

The CEO gave her an approving look that Alena suspected was also tinged with surprise, before agreeing.

'That is true, yes. Which means that it is important to find every new donor we can. From what this one has said to me he is considering making a very generous on-going annual donation to our cause, once he has satisfied himself as to…'

'As to what?' Alena pressed.

Dolores looked slightly uncomfortable.

'Tell me,' Alena insisted. 'I have a right to know.'

'Yes, of course.' Dolores hesitated again, and then told her, 'He has expressed some reservations about the fact that someone so youthful and…and untried will ultimately be in charge of the charity. Because of that he has expressed this wish to meet you personally.'

'To assess my suitability to step into my mother's shoes?' Alena guessed.

'To reassure himself that he is making the right decision,' Dolores corrected her diplomatically. 'Of course if you prefer not to do so then I am sure we could make a tactful excuse—perhaps tell him that you would prefer your brother to deal with the situation?'

Alena weighed up what Dolores had told her. If she met this potential donor and he *didn't* think her capable of stepping into her mother's shoes then she risked losing his support for the charity. It might be safer for her to allow Vasilii to meet him instead. But if she did that how was she *ever* going to be able to convince Vasilii that she was mature enough to take on her mother's role? And, just as important, how was she ever going to feel confident about her ability to do that herself?

She took a deep breath.

'If this prospective donor wishes to meet me, then it is only fair that he does.'

She could see from the CEO's approving look that she had made the right decision.

'If you could set up an appointment with him for me?'

'That's easily done,' Dolores told her with a smile. 'He is actually here now. When I told him that you were coming in this morning, and that I'd speak with you about seeing him, he announced that he would come here to meet you. I did try to put him off, but he insisted, I'm afraid.'

Just as Vasilii would have insisted in the same situation, Alena knew. Such behaviour might be considered by some to be unconventional, but in the world in which her brother moved those men who were the most successful often made their own rules and ignored convention.

'Of course if you want us to tell him that you would prefer him to see him another time...?'

Alena thought swiftly. It was true that already she could feel a frisson of nervous energy jittering through her tummy at the thought of the responsibility she would be taking on in agreeing to meet this would-be donor. But if she wanted to be taken seriously as a woman whose maturity could be relied upon then she had to behave accordingly.

Straightening her spine, she shook her head. 'No. I will meet him now.'

'I was hoping you'd say that. Thank you. This donation would mean such a lot to us. Especially as it would be a regular annual income, guaranteed for the next five years.

We've asked him to wait in the boardroom—
I'll take you there now. And of course I'll be
on hand with you, to answer any technical
questions he might have.'

Alena gave her a grateful look.

The charity's boardroom had windows that
overlooked the street outside. It was decorated in a businesslike and smart colour pal-
ette of off-whites and greys shading to black,
its leather furniture showing subtle gleams of
brushed steel. Its appearance was very much
in accordance with the accepted contempo-
rary look apart from the fact that its table was
round rather than rectangular. It was the photographs displayed on the room's walls that
caught the attention, though: photographs of
children, some of them taken *by* children and
as a result slightly out of focus. They were
haunting, strike-at-the-heart photographs that
told a story of how a girl in the poorest of circumstances could become a young woman
who could hold her head high because of the
education and support she had received from
this charity.

Normally it was to these photographs and
this story that Alena's attention was drawn

whenever she entered this room. Her mother had chosen these photographs herself, and every time she looked at them Alena felt almost as though she could feel her mother in the room with her.

Today, though, it wasn't the photographs that were the focus of her immediate attention. Instead it was the man standing in front of the windows, outlined by the light coming in through them, his features shadowed and hidden. Alena didn't need to see those features to recognise him. Her body and her senses had recognised him immediately. Kiryl.

CHAPTER THREE

AFTER the initial shock, which had frozen her to the spot, a feeling not unlike that she had felt as a child experiencing her first rollercoaster ride raced through Alena, leaving her powerless. Excitement and fear gripped her insides in equal measure, horrified dread fighting with exhilaration as her heart plunged downwards and then soared up again.

Was it merely a coincidence that Kiryl was here? Her heart spun dizzily like a plate spinning clown or a magician. Calm down, she warned herself. Of *course* it was a coincidence. She wouldn't be doing herself any favours as the adult she wanted to be if she allowed herself to think otherwise. Kiryl simply wasn't the kind of man who would try to impress a woman in such a way. Every instinct she had told her that. It *was* simply co-incidence that he was here.

She didn't know whether telling herself that made her feel better or worse. The truth was that she no longer knew what to feel. Or what she actually did feel. He moved slightly, so that the light now fell on him. His expression was unreadable, his green eyes gleaming, and the movement of his body as he came towards her reminded her of the deliberate stalking of a powerful, sleek-muscled hunting animal before it made a controlled leap on its chosen prey.

'Alena, this is Mr Andronov,' Dolores began formally.

'I…'

I know, Alena had been about to say, but Kiryl forestalled her, saying politely, 'Miss Demidova, thank you for finding the time to see me. I appreciate it.'

She felt faint, dizzy, light-headed—as though her body and her senses had been whirled about in a giant fairground machine and then flung into freefall.

Kiryl was reaching for her hand. She had a reactive, defensive, almost childish desire to hide her hands behind her back, so that he couldn't touch her, such was her immediate and intense awareness of what any kind of physical intimacy between them might do to her. Was it only this morning that she had sworn to herself she was in control of her own reactions to him? How deluded she had been.

Dolores was watching her, waiting for her to shake Kiryl's hand. Reluctantly she extended her own, shielding her eyes from his inspection as she did so, not wanting him to read the vulnerability she feared they would betray.

His hand engulfed hers, his fingers strong and warm, curling round it, holding it and her captive. Against her will her body remembered how he had held her the previous day, seeking out the pulse in her wrist and then...

Swallowing quickly against the heady fizz of sensual excitement rushing up inside her, she spoke. 'Dolores tells me that you are considering becoming a donor to our charity.' It was all Alena could manage to say. She must be sensible and mature. She must think not just first but *only* of her mother's charity, and the debt of responsibility she owed it.

'Yes,' he confirmed increasing the tension

she was already feeling when he went on, 'I thought we could discuss the matter over lunch.'

'I...' On the point of saying that she had another engagement, Alena saw the hopeful and pleased look in the gaze Dolores had fixed on her, and remembered that she had told her CEO that she had a completely free day.

'It would give me an opportunity to learn more about the charity and its work—and about your commitment to it. It would be a shame if you were unable to spare the time, as I shall be leaving the country very soon on business.'

Was he testing her? Daring to suggest that she wasn't committed to her mother's charity?

'Yes, of course.' She gave in, adding quietly, 'I am free to have lunch with you.'

'Excellent. I took the liberty of assuming your acceptance and have arranged things accordingly—if you are ready?'

Ready for what? A business lunch, or...? *Stop thinking like that,* Alena warned herself. She must think of this purely as a business exercise—a means by which she could show her half-brother that she was capable of controlling her inheritance. The fact that Kiryl could affect her so dangerously, so sensually, was a vulnerability she must conceal from both him and her brother.

'Yes. Yes, I'm ready,' she agreed, giving Dolores what she hoped was a calm and reassuring smile as Kiryl held open the boardroom door for her. She could see that Dolores looked relieved by her acceptance of Kiryl's request that she have lunch with him. The CEO had indicated that Kiryl's donation was likely to be an extremely generous and ongoing one, and one that they could not afford to risk losing.

To walk through the door she had, of course, to walk past him. The discreet scent of his cologne couldn't mask the scent of him—at least not from her. Her body reacted immediately and intensely to it, her nipples rising into hard peaks of sexual arousal to push impatiently against the constriction of her pretty satin and lace bra. For a dangerous heartbeat she almost lifted her hand to cover her own betrayal, her face flooding with colour as she recognised how easily she could have given herself away.

What was it about this man and *only* this

man that gave him the power to affect her as no other man had ever done? She could feel the wild, reckless surge of her own desire to know the answer to that question, and was equally aware of the far more cautious and conservative side of her nature that urged her not to get involved in a situation that instinct told her she could not control.

It was just a lunch she had agreed to, she reminded herself as Dolores escorted them both to the lift. Nothing more. And a business lunch at that. The fact that he was considering making a donation to her mother's charity *was* merely a coincidence.

But, despite telling herself that, once they were alone inside the lift an impulse she couldn't control had her asking shakily, 'What made you choose my mother's charity for your donation?'

The uncertainty in her voice, combined with the colour coming and going in her face, pleased Kiryl—although of course he was not going to let her see that. It confirmed what his male instincts had already told him, and that was that she was vulnerable to him as a woman. He liked that. He liked it very much indeed. It was time to play with her a little now—to unsettle and unnerve her whilst holding out a tiny piece of bait to tempt her closer.

'You are taking it for granted that I will make a donation—even though I'm sure your CEO has made it clear to you that I am simply contemplating doing so. Isn't that rather dangerous?'

Caught off-guard, Alena could only protest. 'No. I mean, I wasn't taking it for granted. I just meant… I was just curious about why you had chosen my mother's charity.'

'Were you? Or were you perhaps hoping that I had chosen it because of you? Because I wanted to…please you?'

'No!'

The lift had come to a halt and the doors were opening. Hot-faced, Alena was glad of the fact that several other people were waiting to get in. Blindly she stepped out of the lift, her head down, feeling both embarrassed and exposed, stripped bare of her defences. She felt somehow as though he could see right through into the vulnerable heart of her. His penetrating green gaze was far too keen and astute. But then it had probably looked upon many women who had been as sensually aware of him as she was now. Many, *many* women. For her, though, all this was very new—taking her up to the heights and then plunging her down into the depths until she was so shaken up that she felt in danger of losing the power to reason.

Instinctively heading for the main doors to the building, she was brought to a halt when Kiryl reached for her arm, holding it in a firm grip and half turning her towards him. He was standing so close to her that she could feel the power of his male sensuality engulfing her. Like a force-field it surged round her, locked round her effortlessly, holding her captive.

'I am considering your charity because of my own mother.'

His words were so unexpected that it took Alena several seconds to grasp their meaning. Her lungs greedily sucked in the air she had briefly denied them before she was able to question, 'Your *own* mother?'

Good—he had her hooked now. But then, given what he knew about the close relationship she had had with her own parents—especially her mother—it had been a foregone conclusion as far as Kiryl was concerned that to bring his own mother into any conversation he had with her was bound to elicit both her interest and ultimately her sympathy. Right now, though, having piqued her interest, it was best to keep her guessing a little, so Kiryl shook his head.

'This is not the time for such a discussion,' he told her. 'It is something better discussed over lunch. Do you mind riding back in a taxi? Only when I'm in London I prefer to use taxis rather than to have a car and driver following me around. I like the freedom it gives me.'

'No,' Alena assured him, forced into a small self-conscious half-laugh as she admitted, 'I love London taxis. And I'd much rather use them than have a car and driver too.' She pulled a small face. 'Vasilii doesn't understand that, and doesn't really approve.'

It was a small thing to know that he too loved the freedom that being in London gave her. A small thing, and yet immediately it made her feel more relaxed in his company—as though they shared something.

Watching her, Kiryl smiled secretly to himself. He knew perfectly well, from the information garnered by his agent, every single like and dislike Alena possessed. His goal now was to disarm her to such an extent that she ended up trusting him.

Once they were inside a taxi he told her, 'I thought we'd have lunch back at your hotel.'

Alena nodded her head. The hotel did have an excellent restaurant, she knew. The kind of restaurant where important business was conducted on a regular basis. A man's restaurant, Alena often felt, with a menu that was heavy on traditional gourmet meat and fish dishes and portions which she found far too generous. It was silly of her to feel disappointed. This was, after all, a business lunch and not a date. Kiryl was obviously a busy man, just like her brother, and she knew that in similar circumstances Vasilii would have done exactly the same thing.

The reminder to herself that their lunch was a business lunch had her sitting up straight on her own side of the shiny leather taxi seat as she automatically adopted what she hoped was the right pose for a businesswoman.

From his own side of the seat Kiryl, who had relaxed into the darker shadows of the corner of the seat refused to allow himself the mistake of looking at her. Not yet. That would come later. As a boy, running wild with other boys like himself—poor, ragged, half-starved boys, living hand to mouth under the aegis of their elderly foster grandmother, some of them lucky enough to have mothers who worked—he had learned to fish. Sometimes the fish he'd caught had been the only meal there was, so he had had to learn how to take his time and to wait for the right moment to catch his prey unawares.

He knew his silence now was bound to add to the tension he could see Alena was already feeling, and that suited him. Fate had handed the very best wild card he was ever likely to get when it had brought Alena Demidova into his life—without her brother.

The traffic was building up; one of London's many sets of roadworks had brought their taxi to a standstill. Kiryl looked from under his lashes at Alena. His agent had done his work well, and Kiryl knew everything there was to know about her—from the fact that her brother believed her to be currently under the safe care of an elderly ex-matron of an exclusive girls' school to the fact that she was probably still a virgin. He knew all about her parents' marriage, and her English mother's passion for her charity, just as he knew to the last pound how many millions of pounds there were in her trust fund, and how many shares in the businesses of her late father and her half-brother would come into her control when she reached twenty-five.

She was a valuable asset—a valuable pawn, indeed—to the man who controlled her future, and it was no wonder that her half-brother was so protective of her and of her eventual inheritance. With such an asset as his half-sister to barter Vasilii Demidov had a great deal of persuasive power at his command. Via her marriage Vasilii would be able to broker even more power for himself than he already had. There would be many, many men who would want to form an alliance with him via marriage to her. It wasn't her virginity that would be important, either to her brother or the man who married her. It was the power of the alliance that would be created.

He most certainly did not want to marry her. He did not want to marry anyone. But he was quite prepared to let Alena think that he did to win her over.

What he really intended to do was seduce her into falling for him—which would be easy, given the susceptibility to him he had already seen in her and her innocence—and then offer to end their relationship provided her brother backed off from the contract they were competing for. Kiryl's assessment was that *he* was the last person her brother would want as a brother-in-law—a man born not just on the wrong side of the tracks but brought up in the gutters of those tracks. In his judgement her brother would far rather lose one contract than a pawn as valuable as a sister who, married to the right man, would bring far more assets into the family than merely one contract.

He wouldn't like what Kiryl was doing, of course. He wouldn't like it one little bit. But he would have to accept it, because his sister's vulnerability to Kiryl *was* his Achilles' heel. Kiryl had no doubts about that. No man would guard his sister as Vasilii Demidov guarded his unless she was extremely important to him.

And Alena herself… She would have the

sexual pleasure those longing looks she had been giving him said she wanted. And when her brother exchanged her hand in marriage for an increase in his power and wealth she would be able to remember that pleasure when she lay in the arms of a husband she might not particularly want.

Suddenly, out of nowhere, inside his head he could see an image of his mother's face—the anguish in her eyes when she had told him about how she had trusted his father and how he had deserted her and refused to recognise Kiryl himself. He dismissed it as swiftly and ruthlessly as he always despatched any kind of emotional weakness he found within himself.

The taxi pulled off the main road and into the designated drop-off area outside the main entrance to the hotel. Whilst Kiryl paid the driver, a uniformed doorman opened Alena's door for her and helped her out. Following her into the hotel, Kiryl tipped him generously. The man would no doubt remember seeing him with Alena—and that would add further reinforcement to his eventual challenge to her brother either to back out of the contract race or risk seeing his besotted sister marry him.

'This way,' he told Alena, taking a firm hold on her upper arm to turn her in towards the lifts, when she would have walked past them towards the entrance to the hotel's restaurant.

Taking advantage of her confusion, when the lift doors opened he guided her inside it, ignoring the faint resistant stiffening of her body.

'What are you doing?' she demanded. 'I thought we were supposed to be having lunch together?'

'We are,' Kiryl agreed equably. 'But not in the restaurant. I thought it would suit us both better if we had lunch in my suite.'

Suit them both better? What exactly did he mean by that? Alena could feel guilty, excited heat flooding swiftly through her body. Even her face felt as though it was burning with her awareness of how the thought of such intimacy with him was affecting her. And very concerned and wary of that feeling she ought to be, Alena reminded herself as the lift rose swiftly upwards.

Impulsively, her actions driven by sudden

apprehension and the frantic pounding of her heart, she turned to him and told him unsteadily, 'I'm not sure...'

'You're afraid to be alone with me? You think I might try to seduce you?' he guessed. 'Or is it more that you have been wondering what it would be like if I did try?'

'No!' Alena denied immediately.

The lift had stopped. The door was open. He was looking at her with an expression that was a mixture of amusement and something else that re-ignited the desire she had felt earlier.

'Good,' he told her as he guided her out of the lift. 'Because I can assure you that for me this lunch will be strictly business.'

That much was true—even if he had no intention of allowing her to know what exactly that meant.

Torn between relief and embarrassment that he had guessed what was going through her mind, Alena reminded herself that for her the only purpose of this lunch *must* be the fact that she would be able to claim to Vasilii later that she had secured Kiryl's donation to the charity, and that it proved she was mature enough to step into her mother's shoes.

The thick pile of the carpet in the corridor muffled their footsteps as Kiryl guided her towards one of a mere handful of doors in its length, opening it on his suite and indicating that she should precede him into it.

Opposite the entry door to the small rectangular lobby in which she was now standing was a pair of double doors, which Kiryl went to open for her. The sight of natural daylight coming in through the tall windows of the suite's sitting room brought a welcome easing of the tight constriction of her throat, which she was trying to insist to herself had come from the claustrophobic atmosphere of the small windowless space of the lobby.

The decor of the suite's sitting room was familiar to her from staying in exclusive hotels all over the world. Luxuriously comfortable, the room contained everything a demanding guest might need—from a *faux* fireplace with two small sofas either side of it, through to a desk and the large cupboard which she suspected contained a concealed TV set and a mini-bar, and dining chairs placed neatly against one of the walls. The colour scheme of creams and greys was very 'boutique hotel', the fabrics and carpet obviously expensive.

'I'll ring down for our lunch. I hope you'll like what I've ordered. Oh, and there's a guest bathroom through the door off the lobby,' Kiryl informed her.

Alena nodded her head. She was glad about that, of course. She wouldn't have wanted to have to walk through his bedroom to find its *en suite* bathroom. Of course not. She wouldn't have wanted to do that at all. Because if she had she might have looked at the bed—Kiryl's bed—and once she had done that she might have started imagining him lying on it…naked…the magnificent body her senses insisted on repeatedly telling her lay beneath his clothes exposed to her hungry gaze.

By the time she reached the relative sanctuary of the guest bathroom Alena was breathing so heard, her heart pumping so frantically, that she had to lean on the door once she was inside and slowly count to ten inside her head in an effort to calm herself down.

Pulling away from the door, she ran cold water over her wrists to cool her overheated skin, reminding herself of just why she was there. The charity and Kiryl's donation to it. *That* was the only pairing she should be thinking about, she warned herself, quickly reaching for one of the immaculate white linen towels to dry her wrists and hands when she heard the buzzer to the suite and guessed that it was announcing the arrival of their lunch.

And what a lunch!

Alena's eyes widened when one of the two waiters who had wheeled in a hot trolley, along with a table already dressed with a starched white cloth and all the accoutrements one would expect from the most prestigious of restaurants, pulled out her chair for her. The other did the same for Kiryl, and then placed her first course in front of her. Her favourite, she realised as she looked down at the serving of warm pear and goat's cheese salad.

'Thank you—we shall serve ourselves from here.' Kiryl dismissed the waiters with a discreetly given tip, before getting up once they had gone to say, 'A drink first, I think—our national drink to start with.' He removed a bottle of chilled vodka from the ice bucket and poured it into two waiting shots glasses.

'Vodka?'

He was holding one of the glasses out to her across the intimacy of the small table, which was also set with wine glasses, giving her no real option other than to take it. Her fingers had to curl around his as she did so. Why had she never known before this intense difference between her own flesh and that of another? The sensation of his cool, firm skin against hers seared her senses, flooding them with the most acute awareness of him. She could smell the subtle expensive scent of his cologne, fresh and yet somehow at the same time powerfully erotic. He was so close to her that she was sure she could see the dark shadow of the body hair on his chest beneath the fine cotton of his white shirt.

She hadn't taken so much as a sip of her vodka yet, and already she was beginning to feel dizzy and light-headed. Because she knew how important this meeting was—for the charity and for her. Her hand started to shake, and then her body, but to her relief he didn't appear to notice, releasing the glass into her shaky hold before reaching for his own, and toasting her.

'*Za vashe zdorovye*—your good health,' he said, before emptying the glass in one swallow.

Alena knew that she was expected to do the same. It was the tradition to do so. But even though she managed to return the toast, she could only manage to sip at the fiery ice-cold liquid.

'They say it is less intoxicating if you drink it down in one, but I can see that you are a woman who likes to draw out and enjoy her sensual pleasures. And drinking vodka slowly is a very particular sensual pleasure for those who can bear it. One has to withstand its icy cold and then endure its burning heart. Not a task for the faint-hearted—but then I already know that you have a very brave and reckless heart indeed. You have already proved that to me.'

He was smiling at her, his gaze trapping hers and holding it easily with the same strength with which she suspected he would hold her body between his hands if he chose to do so. And surely worse than being trapped was the feeling that in his compelling dark green gaze was a knowing glint that suggested…

Alena didn't want to risk thinking about what it was telling her.

She couldn't help wondering feverishly if his words could *really* mean that he wanted to remind her of his earlier suggestion that she was afraid to be alone with him, when she had denied that suggestion.

'I am referring, of course, to your bravery in meeting the challenge inheriting responsibility for your late mother's charity must place on you.'

Of course he was. Why must she keep on putting a personal slant on everything he said to her? And, even worse, dragging it into the far too overheated sensual awareness of him she should be resolutely ignoring rather than encouraging. He himself was making it plain that his interest in her was not personally biased at all. Was it because she *wanted* him to have a personal interest in her? Because she *wanted* him to desire her and, desiring her, show her that desire? *No.* No—a thousand times no.

'I am proud to take on that responsibility,' Alena assured him, finishing her vodka so that she could break the eye contact he was maintaining with her, hoping she sounded suitably businesslike.

Gesturing towards her starter, Kiryl said, 'I hope the food I have chosen will be to your liking?'

'This is my favourite starter,' she admitted.

Of course it was, Kiryl thought inwardly with cynical satisfaction. He had left nothing to chance about this lunch. He knew exactly what her favourite dishes from the restaurant's menu were.

'You mentioned your own mother when I asked you what had drawn you to my mother's charity,' Alena reminded him, having told herself yet again that this was a *business* lunch—no matter how intimate it might seem. Talking about the charity would help her to focus on that reality. So she wasn't asking him about his mother because she desperately wanted to know more about him. She wasn't.

'Yes, I did,' Kiryl agreed, reaching into the second ice bucket and removing a bottle of white wine, telling her, 'Try this. I discovered it the last time I stayed here and I rather like it.'

Wine on top of the vodka she had already

had to drink; was that really a good idea? For a moment Alena hesitated. It was very flattering to be asked her opinion on a bottle of wine. She wasn't a big drinker—her mother hadn't been, and Vasilii deplored the growing modern trend for young women to drink heavily.

Quickly she placed her hand over her empty wine glass and shook her head, telling him, 'No, thank you. I'm not much of a drinker, I'm afraid. Especially at lunchtime.'

Kiryl put down the bottle and gave her another of those searching looks that seemed to probe the depths of her being.

'Was that decision your own or your brother's?' Kiryl asked.

He was smiling at her again. His smile said that she could feel safe with him, but his words had sliced to the heart of her own growing awareness that a byproduct of Vasilii's protection of her was a certain immaturity when it came to experiencing the things that other girls her age had experienced. Was that how he saw her? As someone immature and inexperienced? A girl rather than the fully sensual and adult woman a man like him was bound to prefer?

'My own,' she answered him. 'Vasilii does not make my decisions or choices for me—nor would he want to do so.'

'So why not allow me to convince you that this wine will greatly enhance your enjoyment of our time together today?'

Her heart was skittering around inside her chest. Another, more experienced woman would know whether or not Kiryl was indulging in flirtatious banter with her with words that were mundane on the surface and yet somehow held a teasing note of a deeper sensuality, but she did not. So surely it would be better to play it safe and assume that it was merely her own over-active imagination that was deepening them with a sensual promise that did not exist?

No sooner had she made that decision than the calming effect it had had on her was ripped away, when Kiryl stood up and came to her side, gently lifting her hand away from her wine glass and continuing to hold it whilst he poured her the merest half a glass of pale straw-coloured wine, before filling his own glass and then returning the bottle to the ice bucket. All the while he continued to hold her hand. And not just hold it. He was touching her fingers, stroking them lightly and almost absently.

'You're trembling,' he told her.

Of course she was. *He* was touching her. No, not just touching her, caressing her, and because of that she *was* trembling—from head to toe—her heart thudding frantically.

'Your brother must be a very stern protector if the thought of having half a glass of wine without his approval can have *this* effect on you.'

He thought she was trembling because she was afraid of Vasilii? By rights she ought to defend her loving half-brother and tell him truthfully that never once in their lives together had she ever, ever had any need to fear him, that it had always been Vasilii to whom she had run with all her troubles, to be comforted by his big-brotherly love for her. But if she did tell him that then he might ask her exactly why she was trembling—and she couldn't possibly tell him that. All she could do was make a mental apology to her brother and try to control the jagged exhaled breath of relief that shuddered through her body when Kiryl let go of her hand and returned to his own chair, lifting his own wine glass to his lips.

'So, tell me more about your mother's charity,' he said.

'You were going to tell me about *your* mother,' Alena reminded him.

For a moment Alena thought he hadn't heard her. He seemed to be looking past her into some dark place that only he could see, a fixed expression on his face.

Was that merely a shadow darkening his eyes, or was it really the ice cold look of anger it seemed?

'I'm sorry,' she apologised uncomfortably.

'For what? Asking about my mother?' Kiryl gave a small shrug, his gaze hardening still further. 'There is no need to be. It is no secret, after all. The reality of my mother's life has been well documented by those who do not thinking it fitting that the son of a homeless Romany should become successful, because that challenges their prejudiced belief in their own superiority and the inferiority of those they choose to label in such a way.'

And that labelling, that rejection and cruelty, had hurt him badly. Alena could tell. Her tender heart immediately ached for him, and for his mother.

'It is true that as a child she did not receive the education afforded to the more privileged in society, but that was not her fault. My father was happy to sleep with her—the beautiful gypsy girl he had seen dancing in a café in Moscow frequented by the wealthy—but the minute she told him that she was pregnant, carrying me, he deserted and denigrated her, saying that she was lying about their relationship and that he had not fathered me. He told her he would rather smother me at birth than acknowledge that he had fathered a child with Romany blood.'

Alena couldn't hold back her gasp of emotion.

'Your mother *told* you about your father's cruelty to you both?' she asked.

A shuttered darkness claimed the light from Kiryl's eyes.

'No. She died when I was eight years old.

But prior to that she told me that she wanted me to know how important love was and how much she loved me. How love could bring the greatest happiness life could hold and the sharpest pain. She wanted me to be proud of what and who I was, even though we were living in the meanest kind of poverty.'

His mother had been a fool—too weak to stand up to his father and demand that he did the right thing by them both. All her talk of love and being proud of himself had meant nothing in the real world—the world that was ruled by men like his father, successful, wealthy men who controlled their own destiny and made the rules by which others had to live. As far as Kiryl was concerned it was far better to focus on that reality than to follow his mother's advice about the importance of love. Look what it had done to her, and through her to him. No, there was no place for love in his life. Love only weakened those who were foolish enough to allow it into their lives.

'So how do you know—I mean about how your father felt about your mother?' Alena asked, wondering if perhaps he had misunderstood the situation. After all, surely no father could ever be so cruel to his child?

'How do I know? I know because my father told me himself, when I finally tracked him down after the woman who fostered me told me the story my mother had told her before she died. My father was a rich man—a powerful and respected man. He told me the truth and then he threw me out on the street outside his grand mansion—like unwanted rubbish, to be swept away out of his sight. I swore then that one day—'

Kiryl stopped speaking, frowning as he recognised how much he had said to Alena. He had never intended to say it, and certainly had never said to anyone else. It was because he wanted to draw her into his plan by eliciting her sympathy towards his mother and making her believe that he had a genuine reason for choosing her charity for his donation, that was why. It certainly *wasn't* because something in her expression and that shocked gasp she had given had somehow unlocked a door within him he had thought safely barred against the burned-out ashes of the pain he kept caged behind that door. It was impossible for any living human being to re-ignite those ashes. They belonged to the promise he had made himself when he had lain in the gutter outside his father's house—that he would prove his superiority by becoming more successful and more powerful than his father had ever been.

His father was dead now, his empire squandered by the second husband of the young wife he had married to provide him with the son she had never conceived for him—the son he had told Kiryl would be the only son he would ever acknowledge.

With the acquisition of this new contract Kiryl would finally succeed in reaching the goal he had set himself as the fifteen-year-old who had gone to Moscow to look for his father and been rejected. That goal had been to create a business empire that was both larger, more profitable and more securely stable than that of his father. Only Vasilii Demidov now stood in his way.

He looked across the table at Alena.

'When I heard about your mother's charity I knew immediately that it was something I wanted to be involved with as a donor.'

That was certainly true. He had known immediately he had read about the charity and Alena's desire to become more involved in it just what a useful tool it would be in winning her trust.

'I know how much work the charity does to help girls have the opportunity to gain an education. I admire you for wanting to take on that responsibility. Many young women in your situation would have handed that responsibility over to someone else.' He flattered Alena warmly.

'I could never do that. The charity was so close to my mother's heart.' She paused, and then said emotionally, 'It must have been so hard for you, growing up without your mother and—'

'According to my father I was lucky that she died, and that I was fostered by a family without the taint of Romany blood.'

Alena felt her throat clog with emotional tears. Within her head she could see that poor baby, and felt a female ache to have been able to hold and protect it. Poor, poor baby to be so cruelly treated by life.

'I was very lucky in having the parents I did,' was all she could manage to say.

'But unlucky, perhaps, in having a brother who is so determined to control your life?'

'Vasilii only wants what's best for me.' She defended her half-sibling quickly.

'For you and for himself, I dare say,' Kiryl responded, adding before Alena could question his words, 'We'd better have our main course before it gets cold. I hope you like Dover sole.'

'Yes, it's another of my favourites,' Alena began as Kiryl reached over to remove her starter, and then guessed, 'You knew that, didn't you? And that's why you've chosen the meal you have?'

So she wasn't entirely without either intelligence or the ability to reason analytically, Kiryl acknowledged. He gave her a small smile and told her, 'Very well—I confess that I did ask the restaurant what your favourite dishes are. I wanted to make a good impression on you.'

Alena couldn't look directly at him. Her heart was singing with delight and disbelief at the thought of Kiryl actually wanting to impress her, and yet at the same time his words had brought her a certain amount of self-consciousness that was making it impossible for her to look at him.

'I'm the one who should be trying to impress you,' she managed to tell him, albeit slightly breathlessly, her voice soft and husky with all that she was feeling. 'After all, I'm the one who has the most to gain from our lunch.'

'Oh, I wouldn't say that,' Kiryl told her softly as he placed her main meal in front of her and removed the cover. 'There is a great deal that I am hoping to gain from our relationship, Alena.'

As he spoke he was looking at her mouth, and as though his look was communicating an unspoken command Alena could feel her lips softening and parting as deliciously sensual ribbons of desire unrolled to flutter inside her with the movement of her breathing.

'Tell me more about *your* mother,' he invited her, abruptly bringing her back to reality, and the fact that this meeting was about her mother's charity and not about the effect he was having on her.

'She was a very special person,' she answered, her voice soft with love for the mother she had loved so much. 'Everyone thought so.'

'Including your half-brother? After all, she was his stepmother.'

'Vasilii loved her very much. He was fourteen when my parents met in St Petersburg, where my mother was working as an English Language teacher at a school there. Vasilii's own mother died when he was seven. He wanted them to marry before they knew that they wanted to marry themselves, so he always says, although my mother used to say that she knew the first moment she met him that she loved my father.

'My mother loved St Petersburg. She and my father used to take me there every winter. It's such a romantic city. A fairytale city with the Neva frozen and the lights of the older quarters twinkling on the snow. It's almost possible to think you're back in the days of dashing young men in the uniform of the Imperial Guard driving their troikas, pulled by a team of three matching horses along Nevsky Prospect, ready to race one another in the morning after spending all night dancing. And then in the summer, when the sun never sets, people flock to party on the islands of the delta. I had dreamed...'

'That you might find love there yourself?' Kiryl suggested.

Alena shook her head.

'I am not such a dreamer that I expect to find love there just because my mother did, but I do think that it would be a very special place to go with…with someone special to me.' That was as close as she was able to get to saying what she meant. Somehow just to speak the word 'lover' in Kiryl's presence was to run the risk of betraying her vulnerability to him, or having him guess that when she said 'lover' she meant Kiryl himself.

Kiryl knew the St Petersburg to which Alena referred—the St Petersburg of the rich and privileged. After all, he was one of them. But he also knew another St Petersburg. The St Petersburg of his own childhood poverty and his rejection by his father. He had turned his back on Russia just as his father had turned his back on him. Kiryl considered himself to be a citizen of the world, not of one part of it.

Not that he was going to say that to Alena. He wanted her to believe that he understood and empathised with her.

CHAPTER FOUR

IT WAS gone three in the afternoon—over an hour since they had finished their lunch and Kiryl had invited her to sit down on the sofa opposite him. Now, as she stood up ready to leave, Alena was feeling dizzy from a combination of the excitement generated inside her at the sheer amount of the donation Kiryl had told her he was going to make to the charity, and the glass of champagne he had insisted they drank to cement that gift.

'You've been so generous,' she told him, wobbling slightly on her heels—no doubt because of the speed with which she had stood up, she assured herself, and not the fact that Kiryl was now standing right next to her, his hand resting supportively beneath her elbow as he walked with her towards the door.

Kiryl had insisted on telephoning the CEO

of the charity himself to tell her of his wonderfully generous donation, before instructing his bank to make the necessary transfer, and since that had somehow or other necessitated the drinking of a second glass of champagne it was perhaps no wonder that she felt a little unsteady and very, very euphoric. But what about those other feelings, clear and sharp, definitely not due in the slightest to her intake of champagne but most unmistakably caused by Kiryl's proximity?

They must be ignored, Alena told herself sternly. They belonged to the rather reckless young woman who had seen him in the foyer and let her hormones dictate her reactions, not the far more sensible businesswoman she had now decided she wanted to be.

Alena started to make a move to the door to the hallway, but Kiryl's hold on her elbow tightened just enough to stop her.

When she turned to him to ask him why he forestalled her, bending his head towards her. Time seemed to stand still, whilst the earth surely rocked beneath her feet. His breath was a warm, sensual touch that caressed her vulnerable flesh. Rivers of sensation flowed from that caress, like the many streams that came with the thawing of Russia's winter, to bring the frozen earth to life once more, freeing it from the icy spell it had been under, melting away its resistance.

'Do you remember saying when we arrived here that you weren't afraid to be alone with me?' Kiryl was asking her.

'Yes…' Her voice turned her confirmation into a small soft moan of self-betrayal. She was standing on the edge of something so very dangerous, and yet so very tempting.

Helplessly her gaze—the gaze she had so determinedly kept removed from his, knowing what she could betray to him if she looked at him—searched for and clung to his. The green eyes were dark with the knowledge of a thousand sensual mysteries that were unknown to her.

'Perhaps you should have been a wise virgin and been afraid after all.'

The sound of his voice—deeper, rougher, strained with something elementally male, his words containing an intimate knowledge of her that she had not thought anyone else shared—made her whole body jerk visibly in response.

He knew she was a virgin? How could he?

Kiryl watched the shadow-play of light and dark dapple Alena's silver eyes, their lucidity as illuminating as St Petersburg's famous 'white nights', when the daylight never truly disappeared. Her lips had parted; the softest pink colour was warming her skin. She was trembling in his hold, held captive by his sexuality and her own response to it.

Her virginity made her an even easier target for the success of his plans. She certainly wasn't a virgin because she was lacking in sensuality, so her chasteness must have been imposed on her—either by circumstance or her brother, or perhaps a combination of both. Kiryl gave a small mental shrug. Why she was still a virgin was immaterial. It simply made it easier for him to overwhelm her sensually and emotionally. For his plan to succeed he needed to convince her that she loved him, and of course that he loved her back. And his plan *would* succeed. It had to.

He lifted his free hand to her neck, gently brushing away her hair so that he could curl his fingers round her slender nape. Her eyes were pure silver now, and brilliant with emotion. Looking into them he told her softly, 'You do know, don't you, that I'm going to kiss you?'

Her heart seemed to jump into her throat, her stomach hollowing with an aching excitement and desire that spilled over into the lower part of her body, making it pulse with a wild surge of longing.

She lifted her hand to his face and touched the skin that was drawn so smoothly over the high cheekbones. Danger glittered in the malachite depths of his eyes, promising a treasure greater than any priceless stone. His breath against her lips commanded them to part still further, and his fingers caressing the nape of her neck under her hair were sending frantic shivers of arousal coursing through her body. Urgency leapt from nerve-ending to nerve-ending within her, spreading like wildfire, until she was possessed by it, the whole of her body one fierce wild ache of need that would not be denied. She wanted this—and him—so badly.

With a small yearning sound she moved

closer to him, offering him her mouth and closing her eyes as she did so.

'No!' Kiryl told her, the word exploding into the sensual tension they were creating. 'No. Don't close your eyes. I want to look into them when I kiss you. I want to watch the pleasure we shall create together being born. Pleasure such as previously you can only have imagined, little virgin. Tell me you want that. Tell me you want me as I want you.'

How could she resist or deny him when every word he spoke only reinforced what she was already feeling? She couldn't—but neither could she find the words to speak her need. Instead she could only press her mouth against his with passionate intensity, feeling them burn against the hard maleness of his before they were taken and possessed, shown and taught lessons of demand and desire and sensuality that were as he had promised her: a world—no, a whole galaxy—away from anything her imagination had ever created.

This need, this desire, this hunger he was creating and feeding inside her was both new to her and yet at the same time had an age-old elemental familiarity that called to all within her that was female. She knew that—and she knew something else as well. She knew that the feelings and needs that were surrounding her and filling her now were being conjured from deep within her by the only man who would ever have the power to call them into life. The only man for her for ever. She knew that so deep within herself that she felt the knowledge must have somehow been born with her, and that he must surely be her destiny.

The stroke of Kiryl's tongue against her own—moving rhythmically, darting, lingering, thrusting with hard demand, then coaxing and teaching her to return the hot intimacy of that caress—set fresh desire exploding inside her. A dazzling banquet of new sensations to experience of which this was only the first course; a thousand new pleasures to know.

Beneath her clothes, her body ached with feverish hunger—her breasts swelling, pushing imploringly against the fabric that denied them the possession of Kiryl's touch. Beneath the ravishment of her senses by his kiss her need brought a soft moan to her throat.

Holding her mouth beneath his own, Kiryl

looked down into her arousal-drenched gaze. Her face was softly flushed, her look pleading, her body quivering like a finely tuned string instrument with the need he had created within it. He could see the outline of her breasts against the fine fabric of the primly buttoned high-necked blouse she was wearing, her nipples stiff and erect. Without saying a word he lifted his mouth from hers and placed it instead over the silk-covered crest of the breast he had cupped with his hand, and then he sucked deeply and hard on it, until she cried out and twisted frantically in his hold, gasping his name with a shuddering breath.

Still without speaking he returned his mouth to hers, nipping sensually at her bottom lip and then thrusting his tongue deep into the soft wetness of her mouth as he covered the now swollen mound of her sex with his free hand and kneaded it rhythmically. Alena clung desperately to him.

'Is this good for you? Is it what you want? Tell me, Alena. Tell me that you want the caress of my mouth against your naked breasts, the taste of your sex against my lips.'

Alena shuddered wildly as his words unleashed shockingly intimate images inside her head, accompanied by unbearably intense surges of desire. With each word he was taking her deeper into a world in which he was her only compass, her lodestar, her only point of rationality, her guide, her leader, her saviour and her all.

'Tell me that you want my touch, my need, my desire for you. Tell me that you want me, Alena,' Kiryl demanded of her.

The sound Alena made was that of a woman aroused to the point where nothing else mattered. She was lost—helpless to resist the surge of biting, devouring, sensual need that Kiryl had conjured up inside her, which had savaged her self-control.

'Yes, I want you,' she told him in small, desperate gasped breaths that pulsated with her arousal and formed the words he wanted to hear. 'I want you. I...'

From her handbag her mobile trilled impatiently, warning her of an incoming text. It dragged her unceremoniously back into the world of reality. She turned towards the sound.

'Leave it,' Kiryl commanded her.

'I can't—it might be Vasilii.'

The grim look that darkened Kiryl's eyes warned her that he wasn't pleased, but Alena knew that Vasilii would worry if she didn't answer his message.

Just the mere act of hurrying over to her handbag brought home to her the changes that Kiryl had already wrought within her body. Each movement reinforced the agonised ache of sensuality that now flooded it. Although he wasn't even touching her Kiryl still possessed her senses, and through them her body. Her breast ached in torment where he had drawn her desire for his touch there to its now frantic throbbing peak. The hot swelling of her sex was something she felt with every step she took. Her whole body shook with the knowledge of how he had transformed her and how much she wanted him. So very much. Now and for always. Part of her was glad.

Her hand trembled as she removed her mobile from her handbag and checked the text, telling Kiryl, 'It *is* from Vasilii.'

As he watched her read her half-brother's message Kiryl saw a small frown pleat her forehead.

'Something's wrong?' he guessed, going over to her.

'Not really. Vasilii says that his business negotiations are taking longer than he expected and he will not now be returning to London for another five days. I was looking forward to telling him in person about your wonderful donation to the charity, but now I'll have to text him instead.'

Kiryl tensed inwardly. The last thing he wanted was Vasilii Demidov getting wind of his presence in his half-sister's life until he himself chose to make him aware of that fact.

'Why not wait to tell him until he returns? Then you can do so and show him the cheque at the same time,' he suggested with a smile.

'Yes. Yes, I will,' Alena agreed. Suddenly she felt acutely self-conscious. Vasilii's text had disrupted the feeling of connection to Kiryl she had had, leaving her feeling uncertain and physically unnerved by the intensity of her sexual response to him. Without the warmth of his arms around her that intensity now felt more than she was able to handle. 'I think I should leave now,' she told Kiryl.

'Running away from me?' he taunted.

It was unfortunate that her brother had texted when he had. It was a very necessary part of Kiryl's plan that he had Alena completely under his spell sexually, and that meant not just arousing her but possessing her as well, winning her total confidence, her total subjugation to him, so that his will mattered more to her than that of anyone else—including her half-brother. It meant giving her the very best sex she could imagine having—or ever would have.

He could take her back in his arms now and make that happen, he knew, but he wanted her to be the one begging for his touch, aching for his possession—demanding it, in fact. And right now he could see that she was too on edge for that to happen.

It wasn't just the disruption and delay to his plan that was affecting him right now, though, he was forced to admit. The immediacy and intensity of his own arousal was causing his body to ache for satisfaction in a way that it hadn't ached in a very, very long time. That desire was the result of his need to succeed in his plan, not any specific desire for *her*, he reassured himself. After all, when had he ever desired any woman to the extent that she made him ache for her against his will? He hadn't, and he never would. It was Alena's own foolish giving, her openly helpless sensual response to him and the fact that she had shown him she had never experienced it that was responsible for the unwontedly fierce surge.

If her brother was responsible for spiking his plans with his text message, then she herself was to blame for the raw ache of need within him that was also disrupting those plans. It was certainly not part of the plan that he should physically want her. A cold, clear mind and a totally controlled body were what he needed. He had invested too much of himself—too much of what he had been and where he had come from, too much of where he wanted to go and what he had done to get there—in the goal he was so close to reaching to risk failure now. Especially not because his body was howling for the possession of one single woman. One single woman who somehow or other had managed to touch the emotional darkness of the vampire within him—that part of himself that somehow remained beyond his control.

Alena was looking tense and clutching her handbag, her manner making it plain to him that she wanted to leave—thanks to her brother reaching out across the ether to claim her allegiance.

'I'll walk you back to your suite,' Kiryl told her, holding up his hand when she started to object. 'Please. It isn't perhaps the correct thing to do to refer to such things, but I believe in plain speaking and I think our afternoon took a turn neither of us was fully expecting. A turn that led a flirtatious kiss to a place that has certainly left me feeling... Well, let's just say that what happened between us touched something within me, and that means that right now I don't want any other man looking at you and guessing what we have just shared. So for that reason you must allow me to be protective and a little possessive and see you safely back to your own door.'

Since he put it like that, how could she possibly refuse?

Five minutes later, escorting Alena along the corridor that led to her half-brother's apartment, after sharing the journey up to it with a uniformed member of the hotel staff whose presence had made any kind of intimate conversation impossible and Alena herself self-conscious, Kiryl recognised that if he was going to be able to seduce her so completely that she gave him her absolute trust, as well as her body, he needed to do so somewhere he could have her completely to himself, where the realities of life and her loyalty to her brother could be banished.

They had reached the double doors to the apartment. If he suggested that she asked him in she would balk at his request, Kiryl sensed, once again mentally cursing the interruption which had meant their intimacy had been brought to an end sooner than he would have liked.

Outside the door, Alena turned towards Kiryl. She had felt acutely self conscious standing in the lift with him under the gaze of the uniformed porter, her body still on fire from the intimacy they had shared. 'Thank you for your donation,' she told him, her voice softening as she added, 'And thank you for telling me about your mother and for letting me talk about mine and St Petersburg.'

St Petersburg. Of *course*! She had already told him how romantic she thought the city, and it would certainly be private at this time of the year, with its elite wealthy citizens having decamped for warmer climates to escape the icy grip of its winter.

Kiryl smiled at her—a slow, warm smile that had Alena's toes curling helplessly into her shoes and the blood beating up under her skin.

'You weren't disappointed, then, in our time together?'

Alena tried to look nonchalant and relaxed, but her heart was thudding so heavily and unsteadily she suspected that he must be able to hear it.

'I...' She shook her head.

'Will it help if I go first and say that I enjoyed every minute of it and I hope we can repeat that pleasure?' Kiryl asked her in a tender voice, and continued without giving her the chance to reply, 'I don't want to rush you or pressure you, Alena, but I don't think either of us was prepared for...for the chemistry between us. It was very special. You are very special. See—you've got me talking and feeling like a raw boy who has never desired a woman before. But then no woman has ever made me feel the way you do.'

That, of course, was true. Because of her connection with Vasilii she aroused in him feelings that no other woman *was* capable of arousing.

'I want to see you again—tomorrow, if you will let me?'

'Yes.' The single word was exhaled on the pent-up breath Alena had been holding. She truly felt as though she was entering a new world—a truly magical world whose axis was Kiryl and the way he made her feel.

'I can hardly bear to let you out of my sight.' Kiryl shrugged and gave a small laugh, as though at the unfamiliarity of his own feelings. And it was true—he *was* reluctant to let her go. But because she was so important to his plans, and not because there was an ache in his groin that said his body had plans of its own for her. A flash of inner irritation rebuked his flesh for its inconvenient and unwanted awareness of her.

'There is so much I want to share with you and show you.'

He made his voice deeper and slightly ragged. And then he discovered that his words were reinforcing—uncomfortably—the surge of desire that had caught him off-guard earlier. His body's rank disloyalty irked him, but he had more important things to deal with right now. After all no man in his thirties worthy of calling himself a man did not know how to control his own sexual arousal.

'So much I want to belong exclusively to us,' he continued softly, 'and to what we're beginning to feel for one another. It's making me selfish. I don't want to share it or you with anyone else. Not yet—not until I know that you...' Deliberately he let his words trail away meaningfully.

And of course Alena knew exactly what he meant. The attraction between them might be compelling and urgent to them, but she couldn't see Vasilii, for instance, seeing it that way. The minute she mentioned meeting Kiryl her half-brother would launch into an avalanche of questions that she didn't want to face. The newness and delicacy of the discovery of their shared feelings needed the privacy of being shared only by the two of them to be nurtured—not exposure to her brother's well-intentioned but potentially over-analytical and forensically intense questioning.

'I feel the same way,' she assured Kiryl. His admission was giving her a new confidence. She was not alone in her desire. They were connected by a mutual need. That was something they shared.

'Then it will to be our secret—for now.'

Alena's keycard had opened the door, which she was holding in one hand. She turned to look at Kiryl, her gaze brimming with the heady joy she was feeling. Still holding the door, she reached out and placed her hand on Kiryl's arm, looking up at him as she did so.

'Thank you,' she told him softly. 'Thank you for the donation to my mother's charity, and thank you most of all for this,' she whispered huskily as she leaned forward and pressed her lips to his.

Taken off-guard by the sheeting feral male need her kiss drove through him, the only thought Kiryl could formulate was illogically angry—didn't she realise that she shouldn't be so open and trusting with him? How vulnerable she was making herself? How open to being used and hurt? But what concern was it of *his* that she might be hurt? When had *he* ever cared about anyone being hurt? Never— and he never intended to care either. That way lay the road to vulnerability and self-destruction. He needed to remain single-minded because it was only by being single-minded that he would reach his goal. And it was only once he had reached that goal that he would finally be able to stand free of the dark shadow of his father's contempt for him and walk away from it.

Pushing her firmly away from himself, he told her truthfully, 'If you don't go inside now you won't be going in alone. And your brother's apartment is *not* the place I want to…'

Alena shook her head, not wanting him to spell out what she knew he meant. Because if he did the effect on her of knowing he wanted to make love to her so badly would make it as impossible for her to leave him as he was hinting it would be for him to leave her.

'Tomorrow,' Kiryl told her. 'Tomorrow I shall come for you, and when I do…'

'When you do I shall be ready,' Alena assured him, bravely and truthfully.

CHAPTER FIVE

SHE was so happy. If she had ever thought before that she had known happiness she had been wrong. That happiness had only been a pale shadow of what filled her now. Filled her and spilled out of her, to surround her with the blissful shining excitement of Kiryl.

She had barely slept, and she'd been up early this morning—adrenalin-filled, and with a surplus of energy that had had her pacing the floor whilst clutching her mobile phone, waiting impatiently for the contact Kiryl had promised her. And that contact *would* come. She knew that. Yesterday had not been some fantasy-fuelled creation of her own imagination. No, it had been real, shared—a commitment made and given to the journey they would make together. A journey to a shared future?

The knifing, twisting, yielding hot sweetness of her emotional and sensual response to that question told her what she wanted, but she was not going to let her hopes run away with her. Instead she was going to live for the moment, for every heartbeat, every touch, every kiss and every intimacy they would share.

The bell to the apartment's security system rang, followed within a second by the ring of her mobile phone.

'Yes?'

'It's me.'

She heard Kiryl's voice in response to her own tremulous answer to the phone's summons.

'I'm outside. Let me in.'

Her hands were all fingers and thumbs as she struggled with the door's lock system, and the small handful of seconds it took her to open the door was a lifetime of impatient longing.

Kiryl swept her up into his embrace the moment the door was open, closing it with a kick of his foot and then leaning back against it whilst he kissed her with all the passion and hunger her own heart felt.

For several minutes the hallway was filled with the soft sounds of Alena's pleasure, the sweetly shocked gasps of her breath and the aching cry of her female delight when Kiryl's hand found her breast beneath the pale grey cashmere of her jumper.

'I want you. I ache so much for you that I have no self-control. All last night I lay awake, thinking what a fool I'd been for not snatching you up there and then and taking you with me. But you—us—what we will have together—deserves far more than the anonymity of a hotel bedroom for its culmination and our shared commitment to it. When we sacrifice our individual selves to become united as one I want it to be somewhere very special.'

Each word Kiryl whispered into her ear, between small erotic kisses bitten delicately into the soft skin of her throat, whilst he caressed her nipple into a tight excited peak of eager surrender, sent a fresh surge of sensual longing and urgency through her. Low down in her body the ache that had merely been tamped down overnight burned hotly into new and impatient life. What he was saying to her, promising her, was lovely—but Alena knew that if he had said he was so impatient that he was going to take her here and now, against the wall in the hallway of the apartment, she would have given herself to him without a second's hesitation.

It made her feel unbearably tender towards him that he should seek to contain their mutual desire in order to give it the right setting, and that feeling increased when he told her, 'I want to make it special for *you*.'

'You are what makes it special,' Alena replied shakily, her voice betraying her emotions. '*You* are special, Kiryl. Special, and wonderful, and…and I am so lucky to have met you.'

Instinctively Kiryl tensed—against both her words and her emotion—wanting to reject them, wanting to tell her that the last thing he wanted from anyone was an emotional connection. Emotional connections had no place in his life. They never had and they never would. He had learned young that it was safer to shut himself away from his emotions. Except, of course, those that drove him to obliterate the memory of his father's rejection by achieving for himself what his father had not been able to achieve.

Alena's open vulnerability irritated him like a piece of grit in his shoe, demanding his attention even though he didn't want to give it. It had been her parents' responsibility to prepare her for the harsh realities of life. Now it was her brother's. If they hadn't taken care to do that then why should it irk him so much? Especially when her vulnerability was the foundation on which he was building his plans to win that all-important contract.

What was it that was *really* causing his irritation? Surely not his conscience? Kiryl shrugged aside that thought. He did not have a conscience—not where the all-important task he had set himself was concerned. So why the irritation? After all, it would make things far more difficult for him if she were suspicious of him and his motives.

And, no matter how ready she might be to let him see how she felt about him *now*, she would be more than suspicious, a few weeks from now, when he walked away from her with his prize, leaving her with her dreams and her pride shattered.

Kiryl tensed his mind against his own thoughts. Her future pain was no concern of his. *She* was no concern of his. She had her rich, protective brother to take care of her, and she had grown up with loving parents. The contrast between their childhoods couldn't have been greater. She a child born of a union between two people who had loved one another and who would no doubt have welcomed the birth of a child to celebrate and cement that love. He a child born of a union rooted in abuse and contempt on the part of his father and gullibility on the part of his mother—a child loathed by his father and abandoned by his mother, who had died leaving him unprotected.

Kiryl frowned. He didn't want to be dragged back to the pain of his childhood. It was over, after all, and he had severed every link that had ever connected him to it. He had re-invented, recreated himself as the man he was now. A man proud to say that his mother had been a Romany and that he had the gifts, the skills, everything he did have, to become what he now was. Unlike Alena, he had had no advantages to help him through life, but he had still been able to achieve his goals. Almost.

'I've arranged a surprise for you,' he told her.

'A surprise? What kind of surprise?' Alena demanded.

'The kind that requires a passport. You do have a passport, I trust?'

A passport? He was taking her away somewhere? Alena's heart leapt. 'Yes, of course,' she agreed. 'But…'

'No more questions,' Kiryl told her autocratically, before looking pointedly at his plain, discreetly expensive gold watch, its strap glinting warmly against the sinewy strength of the tanned flesh of his wrist.

Kiryl had good hands—strong hands. A man's hands, with lean fingers and clean, well-kept unmanicured nails.

'I'll give you five minutes in which to make your choice—either to say yes and come with me or to say no and stay here.'

'Five minutes? But…'

'Trust me, Alena,' Kiryl told her fiercely. 'Trust what you feel and trust *me*. Perhaps what happened between us yesterday happened too fast—for both of us. But passion—a man's passion for a woman and hers for him—can be like that… That doesn't make it wrong.' His voice dropped to become hauntingly low as he told her thickly, 'Nothing we share together could ever be wrong. All I want is the opportunity to prove to you how very special you are to me…how very special we can be together. And for that we need privacy and somewhere very special. If you will let me take you there.'

The colour came and went in Alena's face. She knew the 'there' that he was talking about wasn't just the 'there' of his surprise destination; what he was saying to her—what he was promising—was that he would also take her to the heights of sensual pleasure and fulfilment. Her head was spinning, her heart racing, her body aching with impatient longing. The choice was hers. He had told her that. She could refuse. She could tell him that she needed more time, that she needed more information. But Alena knew that she wasn't going to. Overnight she had grown from a girl who had felt nervous uncertainty yesterday about whether she was strong enough for her own passion to a woman who now knew beyond any doubt that she was—and how much she wanted him.

She took a deep breath, and then asked him in a voice that only trembled very slightly, 'What will I need to pack?'

'Very little.'

When Alena's face went bright red and she dropped her lashes over her eyes Kiryl laughed. He had been so intent on his plan that he had forgotten for a minute how inexperienced she actually was.

'Ah, I see,' Kiryl teased her. 'You are imagining that I plan for you to wear only the minimum amount of clothing?' He shook his head. 'That was not what I meant at all. I should have said that you need only pack a few essentials. The rest we will buy when we reach our destination.' He paused, and then told her softly, 'Besides, when I make love to you it will not be "very little" you will be wearing, it will be only your own skin—because the only covering you will need will be my hands, my touch, my kiss and my body.'

Now her face was hotter than ever—and so was her body. The images conjured up by

Kiryl's words were so enticing and exciting that they made her feel giddy with longing.

'You have three minutes left,' Kiryl reminded her. 'And don't forget your passport.'

'But I need to know something,' Alena protested. 'Are we going somewhere hot or…?'

'We are going first to the airport, and for that you will need a coat. More than that I am not prepared to tell you.'

He was looking at his watch again.

The sudden reality of how awful it would be if he were to leave without her was the only impetus Alena needed to send her almost running into her bedroom. She stood for several vital seconds, too ecstatically happy to be able to formulate a single practical thought, until she remembered how little time she had.

'A few essentials' Kiryl had said, Alena reminded herself as she hurried into her walk-in wardrobe-cum-dressing room and removed a case, quickly sweeping her toiletries into it and then equally speedily opening a drawer to remove a couple of sets of clean underwear, grabbing her passport from her dressing table drawer to put it into her handbag and then reaching up for a quilted dark grey parka that toned with her pale grey cashmere jumper and silk taffeta skirt. Bending down to kick off her heels, she dropped them into a bag before putting them into the case and then slipping on a pair of warm lined boots.

'Four minutes,' Kiryl told her when she re-emerged into the sitting room with her case. 'That's one minute too many. For which I shall demand that you pay me a forfeit, so be warned,' he teased her, looking pointedly at her mouth in a way that told her the forfeit he had in mind was going to be a kiss.

'You've got your passport?' he asked, holding out his hand, his manner suddenly briskly businesslike.

Alena nodded her head, automatically reaching into her handbag and passing it to him. When their fingertips touched Alena felt her whole body tingle in sensual excitement from that brief contact. And if that brief contact could have that kind of effect on her, then how was she going to feel when he really made love to her?

'Come,' Kiryl commanded, holding his hand out to her after he had tucked her passport away in an inside pocket of the cashmere overcoat he had previously been carrying but which he was now wearing over his suit.

Just for a second Alena hesitated, suddenly sharply aware of the symbolism of what taking his hand would mean—of the giant step she would be taking, leaving behind her the security of her brother's loving protection to go with a man who until yesterday had been a stranger to her. A stranger who now held her heart, Alena reminded herself. A stranger to whom she felt more intimately and emotionally connected than anyone else she had ever known. A stranger who was, she was sure, the one to whom she was destined to give her heart and herself.

So not a stranger after all, but her one true love. Once she had given her hand—herself—to Kiryl she would have given them for ever, she knew.

The smartly uniformed young steward waiting for Alena at the top of the stairs into the private jet with its discreet corporate logo—Kiryl's corporate logo—smiled welcomingly at her as he showed her into the luxuriously appointed cabin, whilst Kiryl spoke with the captain.

'We're cleared for take-off,' the steward told her, stowing her small case in what looked like a wall but was in fact a bank of cupboards, 'and as soon as we're airborne I'll be serving pre-lunch champagne and canapés. This is the control for your seat,' he added, showing Alena a control unit. 'If you'd like me to show you how to use it?'

Alena smiled politely and shook her head. She was no stranger to travelling by private jet—her brother owned one, after all—and she had recognised the private area of the airport the minute the chauffeur-driven limousine that had picked them up from the hotel had turned into it.

The interior of this one might be slightly smaller than her brother's—Vasilii travelled extensively all over the world—but it was every bit as luxurious, if not more so. The expensive plain grey carpet with its black stripe was thick and immaculate, the leather of the charcoal-grey leather chairs so soft that Alena couldn't resist stroking her fingertips along the arm of her own.

This section of the cabin was furnished rather like a small meeting room, with its leather chairs and a sofa, but a door in the dark glass screen at the rear of the cabin caught her attention.

Seeing her look at it, the steward told her, 'The door leads to Mr Andronov's workstation area, and beyond it are the bathroom and the galley. If I may take your coat for you?'

Nodding her head and returning his smile, Alena allowed him to help her off with her coat. He was a good-looking young man, with a certain look in his eyes when his gaze brushed her body that told her he was attracted to her.

Kiryl, who was on the point of entering the cabin, saw the way the steward looked at Alena as he took her coat, and the sudden, sharply savage red burn of male possessiveness that took him from the doorway to Alena's side was so swift and overwhelming, so instinctive, that it had dictated his actions before he could even think of defying it.

It was, he told himself, perfectly natural—given the importance of the success of his plan. And, given Alena's naïveté, he wanted to ensure that no other man showed appreciation of her. His response had been driven by practicality, that was all. Practicality. Not male possessiveness, and certainly not male jealousy.

'You still haven't told me where we're going,' Alena reminded Kiryl when he took his own seat preparatory to take-off.

'No, and I don't intend to tell you. It's a surprise, remember?'

'But you can tell me how long the flight will be?' Alena suggested coaxingly.

'Around seven hours,' he told her promptly. 'And seven hours could take us to many places. New York—one of the most vibrant cities on earth—Oman, or Dubai, where so many Russians love to go in the cold weather.'

Alena laughed. 'Vasilii certainly loves it there. He hates the cold. His mother's family tribe came originally from the desert.'

'Then there is the Caribbean,' Kiryl continued.

'You could always simply tell me where we are going instead of keeping me guessing,' Alena pointed out.

'Ah, but if I did that what would you have to think about for the next seven hours?' Kiryl asked softly.

His words might sound innocent but Alena knew that they were not—just as she also knew perfectly well exactly what was going to be occupying her thoughts for the next seven hours. And that would not be their destination so much as what would happen when they reached that destination. Kiryl holding her, touching her, taking her to bed and making her his. Kiryl, Kiryl, Kiryl. He was her journey and her destination.

Seven hours later, after an elegant lunch of smoked salmon followed by sea bass served with perfectly cooked vegetables and then champagne and orange mousse, Kiryl had flirted with her so subtly that some of the time she hadn't been sure if he had really said or intimated what she had thought he was saying, or whether it was her own fevered longing and imagination that had made her believe his words cloaked a deliberately sensual message and the promise of shared pleasures to come.

One glance out of the jet's window as they

started to descend told Alena exactly where
Kiryl was taking her. Her face alight with joy
and excitement, she turned to him to exclaim
happily, 'St Petersburg! Oh, Kiryl. Thank you.
You remembered what I said about it.' Impulsively she reached out to him, her hand on his
arm, her face turned up towards him.

As he looked down at her the sudden savage
ache of physical desire that gripped his body
shocked Kiryl into immobility. *She* was the
one who had to want *him* so unbearably that
her need was impossible for her to resist—not
the other way around.

He reached out to push her away, but a sudden movement of the plane caught them both
unaware, jolting Alena so that she lost her bal-
ance and fell against him, leaving Kiryl with
no alternative other than give in to his instinctive male response to protect by taking hold
of her. And once she was in his arms his body
reacted to her presence there as though it was
something it had hungered desperately for.

Need surged against the barriers of his self-
control, its urgent arousal hardening, its ache
for so much more than the feel of her mouth

beneath his as he took it in a kiss that was far more intense than he had wanted it to be.

As their jet descended from the clouds to what for Alena was the most beautiful winter city in the world, it wasn't St Petersburg that captured and held her attention but Kiryl himself. The hot, passionate swiftness with which he had taken her mouth thrilled and delighted her, and answering arousal rose up inside her to make her strain eagerly and urgently against Kiryl's openly hardened body. His tongue caressed her own in moves as fiercely sensual and urgent as the most explicit of intimate tangos.

It wouldn't have mattered where he had chosen to bring her, Alena acknowledged. What mattered—*all* that mattered for her—was being with him. The landscape of her dreams and the city of her heart was now Kiryl himself.

CHAPTER SIX

'THIS is your room, so I'll leave you to make
yourself at home here before we have dinner,
which I've arranged to be served in an hour's
time.'

'My room?'

Alena was conscious of the fact that she had
barely spoken since the helicopter waiting for
them at the airport had dropped them off here,
on one of the many small islands in the delta
of the Neva, and Kiryl had shown her into a
house so perfect that she had only been able
to stand and gaze in delight at its fairytale interior.

Obviously dating back to the time of the
early eighteen-hundreds, from its exterior architecture, the house was a perfect jewel of its
era. All she had been able to say, after taking
in its soft sugared-almond-blue-painted exte-

rior and the elegance of the interior, had been, 'This house is so beautiful! Is it yours?'

Kiryl had shaken his head. 'No, I've rented it,' he'd answered her.

Now, though, Kiryl had shown her up to a beautifully decorated guest suite with overtones of French Empire style. His reference to the room being her room had caused her to turn and look at him in confused uncertainty. She had assumed that they would be sharing a room—that the bed she would sleep in would be Kiryl's bed. She had no past experience to guide her, to tell her what to say or do. No protection against the cold slamming weight of the disappointment and sense of loss that struck her.

Kiryl saw the uncertain and disappointed look Alena gave him, and then the bed. It was an important part of his plan that *she* should be the one to want *him*, to commit to him willingly and through her own choice. Now, easily able to read her mind, he asked softly, 'You expected that we'd be sharing a room?'

'Yes,' Alena answered him honestly, marvelling yet again at the ease with which he seemed able to read her mind, and the way that created a very special bond between them.

'That must be your wish and your choice,' Kiryl said. 'I have practically kidnapped you and brought you here, but the choice, the decision to continue the journey I began, must rest with you. It will be for you to decide whether or not you wish to invite me to your bed or exclude me from it. That is why I have given you your own room. This is my gift to you. Should you choose to give yourself to me that will be your gift to me, given freely.'

The emotional chord struck deep within her by Kiryl's words brought Alena close to tears. He was so special, so wonderful, so perfect— and so everything she wanted.

'Tonight we will have dinner here, and I warn you that over dinner I intend to do my utmost to make you want what I already know I want so very desperately,' Kiryl continued. 'But if at the end of the evening I have not succeeded, then...'

The look he was giving her would surely have caused ice to burst into flames, Alena thought dizzily.

'Then there is always tomorrow, and all the

tomorrows after it, until you decide that you are ready for me.'

She wanted him. She wanted him so badly. His tenderness towards her and the way he had expressed that tenderness made the whole of her ache with love for him. She had always secretly dreamed of a man who would arouse her sensuality until her need for him was beyond her own control and yet at the same time be so noble that she would know she could trust him even when she could no longer trust herself. But she had never expected to find one.

'You are the missing piece that will complete my life, Alena. I believe that more strongly than I have ever believed anything.'

He was only speaking the truth—even if that completion referred to a goal that had nothing to do with loving her, Kiryl acknowledged inwardly. He had no place for love in his life. Love made men vulnerable, and the vulnerability he had experienced as a child had left him determined never to be vulnerable again—to anything or anyone.

'You are my destiny, Kiryl,' Alena responded, her voice choking with emotion.

'And I want control of that destiny to lie in

your own hands,' Kiryl told her, holding her gently as he bent his head to kiss her on the forehead.

She was alone in her suite. Alone and yet not alone. She would never be alone again because of Kiryl. She could smell the scent of his skin, hear the sound of his voice inside her head, feel her body kick into excited, aching longing at the thought of his touch.

Her mobile phone chirruped—an incoming text.

Reaching for it, she felt a small pang of guilt when she saw that it was from Vasilii. Vasilii, who thought she was in London—in his apartment. But there was no need for her to feel guilty, she assured herself. After all Vasilii would not dream of telling *her* if he was spending time with a woman. She was an adult, with every right to keep her private life private. When Vasilii did get to know about Kiryl he would like and admire him, of course. How could he not do so? He would be relieved, too, that she had given her love to someone he could respect—someone who shared his business values and his hard-working mindset.

Vasilii had no time for playboys and the like—young men with wealthy fathers who had no need to earn their own living. If anything, he despised them. But even they didn't merit the degree of contempt her brother felt for the kind of fortune-hunting young men several of the girls she had been at school with had become involved with—Z-list celebrities in the main, who had attached themselves to the girls at one or other of London's hot nightspots. Such liaisons damaged the reputations of the girls concerned and that of their families, Vasilii had told her. Her half-brother held certain somewhat old fashioned views about family reputations. Their father had often teased him that those views came from Vasilii's mother's family and its nomadic warrior traditions, where family pride and good name was so very important.

Her text back to her brother assured him that she was all right, and then she looked at her watch. In forty-five minutes she would be dining with Kiryl—which meant that she had better hurry up and have a shower…although of course she had nothing to change into. Tomorrow she would be able to buy herself something from the expensive and exclusive designer shops on Nevsky Prospect, but for now she would have to continue to wear her cashmere jumper and taffeta skirt.

Guessing that the double door in the wall next to the room's huge king-size bed must lead into the bathroom, Alena opened them— to discover that a dressing room lay beyond them, with another pair of double doors on the far wall, which were standing open to reveal the bathroom. As she walked towards it a note stuck to one of the doors of the dressing room's wardrobes caught her eye. Pausing to look at it, she read, 'Alena—open me.'

Hesitantly she did so—only to stare at the contents of the wardrobe in delighted amazement. Hanging from the rails were the clothes she had bought at the beginning of the winter season from her favourite London shops. Or rather brand-new versions of what she had bought, Alena recognised as she looked at them more closely. Brand-new and in her size.

Kiryl had organised this, she marvelled. But how? How had he known exactly what she had bought for herself? Bemused, and torn between laughter and disbelief, Alena checked through the clothes hanging there, clutching the skirt of the silk dress she had only minutes before been wishing she had with her to wear this evening. Releasing the dress, she pulled open one of the drawers—her favourite underwear, all discreetly tissue-wrapped, and in another drawer her favourite toiletries.

Ten minutes later, after a quick shower, she removed the cream silk dress from its padded hanger. She had fallen in love with the dress the minute she had seen it in the shop, but now it wasn't excitement about the dress that made her hands tremble as she slipped it on over the nude satin and lace underwear she had changed into. No, it was Kiryl who was responsible for her excitement—her excitement and her longing to be with him.

Exactly on the dot of the hour Kiryl had given her, just as she had finished misting the air around her with her favourite scent, there was a knock on her bedroom door.

When she opened the door to find Kiryl standing outside, immaculately and formally dressed in a dark fine wool suit, as though he had known that she would choose to wear something formal herself, all she could do was shake her head and gesture to her dress.

'How…?'

'Magic,' he teased, refusing to say any more as he offered her his arm with old-fashioned courtesy.

'I can hardly believe all this is really happening,' Alena murmured in delight as he escorted her downstairs.

'Believe it,' Kiryl told her as they crossed the marble hallway and then went through the drawing room to the dining room beyond, where an immaculately dressed waiter was already pulling out a chair for her at a table dressed with what was obviously expensive china and crystal.

Half an hour later, when they had been served with a first course of caviar and Kiryl had insisted on them toasting one another with champagne, Alena gazed at him in adoration.

'You've made everything so perfect—St Petersburg, this house, my clothes. I can't imagine anything that could be better than this.'

There was a small telling pause, during which Kiryl looked into her eyes and then let his gaze slip to her lips and stay there.

'I hope that's not out true,' he said softly. 'Because I can assure you that I can—and I hope that before tonight is over it won't just be in our imaginations that we will have experienced it.'

Alena made a soft murmured sound and took a gulp of her champagne. She wanted Kiryl so much—far more, in fact, than she wanted her dinner. Far, far more. She wanted him so badly right now that...

She put down the forkful of food she had been about to eat, the excitement squirming in the pit of her stomach melting into a heated longing.

'What is it?' Kiryl asked, indicating the food she had put down. 'You aren't eating.'

'I'm not hungry,' Alena responded, bravely lifting her gaze to meet his as she added huskily, 'At least not for food.'

Kiryl looked at her for so long without saying anything that Alena wondered if he had understood what she meant—or, even worse, if he did understand but disapproved of her being so direct. She was in such new and unfamiliar territory here. She wouldn't have wished away the happy times she had spent in her teens, being so close to her parents that it had been their company she had wanted rather than that of her peers, but not for the first time since she had met Kiryl she was regretting her sheer lack of worldly experience.

For a handful of seconds Alena's directness kept Kiryl still in his chair. He was used to women coming on to him in the most blatant and openly sexual of ways, just as he was familiar with the ploys they used when they wanted to appear more subtle, but the sheer open honesty of Alena's words, combined with her uncertainty, touched and then released something within him—a sudden pang of something approaching protective tenderness. A protective tenderness that had no right to be there and that he certainly did not *want* to be there, he warned himself as he fought against it.

Another unfamiliar and equally unwanted feeling followed hot on the heels of the first one—this time the knowledge that he could stop now, turn his back on his plans, let her down gently and make it easy for her to walk

away from this and him with only her heart
bruised.

Give up his plans? His goal? The entire
raison d'être that had dictated the whole of
his adult life? For what? To save a woman
who meant nothing to him from pain? Was
he going mad?

Angry with himself, Kiryl deliberately ignored the choice presented to him. There was
only one road he wanted to follow, and that
was the road he had mapped out for himself
all those years ago.

Why didn't Kiryl say something? *Anything?* The longer he remained silent the more
Alena's heart rocked sickly inside her chest,
and the conviction that she had somehow mis-
read the situation—that the desire she had
thought he had for her was merely created by
her own imagination—strengthened.

But then he removed his linen napkin from
his lap, crushing it in his hand before he placed
it on the table and then stood up. Watching
him walk towards her, Alena held her breath,
her heart thumping heavily inside her chest.

Kiryl reached down to take hold of her
hands and gently pull her to her feet, demand-

ing with heart-shaking urgency as he did so, 'You mean that?'

The relief that coursed through her was mixed with heady excitement and a fierce longing that sent its message of arousal coiling and pulsing through her lower body.

'Yes. Oh, yes.' Her voice shook as she whispered the words to him.

It was triumph in the success of his plan that was filling him with the emotions that were racing through him now, Kiryl assured himself. It was desire for that success that was causing his blood to pound through his veins and his heart to pump so fast. Not any real desire for her. The mental images and the physical awareness of how it would feel to have her naked body beneath his touch and his mouth meant nothing. They were simply his body's way of translating all that the success of his plans meant to him. There was no personal significance in those images, just as he did not feel any personal desire for her. That was impossible and non-allowable.

But knowing that did not mean he must not convince her that he wanted her—and not merely wanted her but ached and yearned for

her and her alone. Each touch between them—
each breath, each look and every single caress—must carry that message to her. And that
was why he must make love to her as though
she was his everything, his all.

Keeping his gaze fixed on Alena's, Kiryl
lifted her champagne glass to her lips and
commanded softly, 'Drink.'

Slowly Alena did so, her hand trembling as
she placed it over his around the stem of the
glass. Her gaze was molten silver with arousal
when she raised it to him, her whole body
shuddering with mute longing when he drank
from her glass himself, so that the kiss with
which he took the sweet gasp of frantic need
from her lips tasted of champagne and then
of him. Its sensuality rocked her back on her
heels, leaving her needing his arms around
her to steady her as he placed the glass back
down on the table.

If the slow and deliberate building intensity
of his kiss had been a master class in subtle
arousal—not that her desire for him needed
to be coaxed or husbanded—the sensation it
caused inside her was nothing to the shock-
wave of erotic response that flooded through

her when Kiryl demanded, 'Have you any idea how close I am to taking you right here and now? How knowing that makes me feel? Have you any idea just how dangerous you are to me and my self-control? How you've occupied every single one of my thoughts since yesterday?'

His words so closely echoed what she herself was feeling that Alena was left unable to speak, never mind control the fireworks of savagely sweet pleasure they sent exploding through her body.

'I want to take things slowly—to give you time to think about what you want—to listen to reason and logic, not my senses—but right now... I want you so much. And I have to warn you that if we leave this room now I can't promise to let you go when we reach your bedroom door. So unless that's what you want—unless I am what you want—'

'You *are*. You are *all* I want,' Alena insisted passionately.

Kiryl could feel her tremble in his arms beneath the force of her words, and his own body ignited in a surge of fierce male pleasure in its knowledge of her sexual desire for him. And only because of that. Not because against his own mental will he wanted her with something that was dangerously close to going beyond logical reason. That was something he was going to refuse to hear.

Somehow Kiryl managed the transition from dining room to the door of her bedroom with such delicacy that Alena had no real awareness of them having made it apart from the fact that they were now here, outside her door.

Kiryl's arm was binding her to his side as he turned her towards him, his free hand smoothing the hair back off her face as he warned her, his voice a raw low sound against her ear, 'You must send me away now if you want me to go, sweet Alena. How well named you are—as irresistible to me as Helen of Troy was to Paris. I am no more capable of giving you up than he was her.'

'I don't want you to give me up.' Alena trembled valiantly against the storming assault of her own longing as he pushed against the barriers of her inexperience, melting them with his heat. 'Come with me, Kiryl,' she begged as she reached for the handle to her bedroom door. 'Come with me and show me...teach me... All I want is you. All I will ever want is you.'

The bedroom door was open, standing as wide as the door to her heart and her sensuality, and yet instead of stepping forward to seize the prize he wanted Kiryl found that he was standing still, held to the spot by an alien emotion that gripped him as tightly as though a boa constrictor had coiled itself around his mind.

Why was he hesitating? This was a vitally important step along the road to the fulfilment of his plan—more important, perhaps, than any of the other steps he had taken. Bold, invincible steps that had taken him easily through the ruins of other men's attempts to stop his successful financial progress. If he had crushed them beneath his will-power then why was he hesitating now, when all he had to do was simply take what was being offered to him? Surely he wasn't afraid of doing that? Afraid that the very act of taking what Alena was offering might also take from him something he had no desire to give? Afraid that somehow the taking of her heart would demand a price that would ultimately prove too heavy for him? Afraid to step over the entrance to her room because of what doing so might reveal to him about himself?

Never.

Bending down, he swung Alena up into his arms and claimed her mouth in a kiss that committed him to his chosen course of action, sealing behind him all the doors he had thrust open to get to the place where he now was.

CHAPTER SEVEN

THEY were in her bedroom, the lights turned down low by the unseen, highly efficient staff who must have come in whilst they were having dinner to prepare her room for the evening. In the soft light the green darkness of Kiryl's eyes as he fixed his gaze on hers set Alena's heart beating suffocatingly fast. Having placed her on the bed, Kiryl was now sitting beside her, looking down at her. He reached out and covered the wild beat of her heart where it was lifting the soft silk of her dress.

'So much excitement,' he whispered against her throat. 'I hope I will not disappoint you.'

'I am the one who is more likely to disappoint you,' was Alena's unsteady response.

'That is not possible. It is for me to light the way for you, so that your desire is mine, your pleasure mine and your satisfaction mine,' Kiryl responded.

He was kissing her again—slow, delicate kisses that he trailed from her collarbone to the corner of her mouth and then back again, gently at first, and then with an urgent rhythmic tempo that accelerated the beat of her heart and had her digging her fingers into his shoulders in an increasing urgency of need.

The hot satin touch of male hands on her body, swiftly removing her clothes, replacing them with boldly sensual kisses, made Alena feel as though a river of molten desire was sweeping away whatever hesitancy and inhibitions she might have had along with her garments.

Soon it wasn't enough just to have Kiryl touching her, and she was the one reaching for him with trembling, eager fingers, tugging at buttons and cloth, belt and zip, until the lamplight burned golden against the magnificence of his torso, soft with dark body hair. No shadows were deep or dark enough to conceal the naked aroused thrust of his maleness—a maleness that evoked a female desire within her as primitive as his.

Lost in a world filled with awed delight and an aching need to know the reality of his possession, Alena reached out towards him, her hot gaze embracing the thick fullness of his erection, her fingertips trembling slightly as she touched it in a hesitant exploration that grew bolder with the hot flood of delight that flowed from where she was touching him right through her body to her own eager sex.

The unsteady breath she exhaled brushed the soft hairs on Kiryl's skin, releasing him from the dangerous spell her touch had put him under with its combination of open female longing and inexperience. Kiryl frowned. Something was happening to him. Thoughts and feelings were growing inside him that he didn't want—like the knowledge that this was the first time she had touched a man in this way, and that the responsibility for how she would view the pleasure of sex—or the lack of pleasure—potentially for the rest of her life lay with *him*.

Whilst he hesitated Alena explored him intimately, her breasts swelling with female ecstasy in his maleness, her nipples tight and thrusting, the ache deep down within her sex growing and pulsing into a clamour of female need. Overwhelmed by the intensity of her own desire, she leaned forward and touched her lips to the engorged head of his sex.

Like winter ice on the Neva, cracking under the force of the sun's warmth, Kiryl felt the shock waves of her intimate touch crashing through him. Feelings, needs he was totally unable to control burst into turbulent boiling life inside him. Alena was in his arms, her naked body shimmering satin against the bed, her hair spread all around her in a tumble of rich gold, her nipples burned to the deep, dark heat of eagerness. Her thighs were splayed apart and the soft delicate line of blonde hair on her sex was dancing in the light as her hips rose and fell in a writhing agony of need. The same need that was thudding through his own body, like a pile driver sending its insistent message, making its unstoppable demand for that the soft, wet velvet intimacy that would take it and hold whilst he drove them both to the heights and kept them there.

A raw sound escaped from Kiryl's throat just before he bent his head to take her nipple between his lips, to rake it with his teeth in an agony of male desire that had what was left of her self-control splintering into a hundred thousand shards of aching longing. It ricocheted through Alena's own body. It was a sound of denial and demand, of agonised longing and the desire to resist that longing, of a need that could not be controlled or contained, and it echoed everything that she felt herself. It was the cry of his heart and her own heart, was crying back to it.

Kiryl told himself that he must remember this was her first time—that he must make her pleasure so great that what she so obviously felt for him now was intensified. He must and he would—but still an inner voice warned him that, despite the importance of that, it was surely not really necessary for him to slide his hand the silky-smooth length of her inner thigh and feel the responsive quiver not only of her flesh there but of her whole body, for him to follow that caress with the exploration of his mouth. But he was doing it, and he didn't want to stop—couldn't stop—even though Alena had tightened her fingers into his skin and was begging him to stop. Because she could not endure the intensity of the pleasure he was giving her.

It shocked him that those throaty, sobbed words, driven with female arousal and never heard by him before, could have such a savagely erotic effect on him. No other woman he had ever known had revealed a helpless inability to withstand the desire he aroused in her so openly or so honestly, and certainly no other woman had said to him as Alena was saying now, 'But I want to please you. I want to hold you and touch you and...'

Kiryl's hand cupped the softly swollen flesh of Alena's sex as he kissed the top of her thigh. His fingers stroked apart the deep pink flushed lips that guarded what lay beyond them.

'This pleases me,' he told her truthfully, his own voice thickened by what he told himself was his satisfaction in her desire for him. 'Your response to me, your desire for me, the sweet hot wetness of you here, where you welcome my touch and make those little sounds of need you are making now, please me, Alena. This...'

His thumb stroked slowly along the moist,

sensitive valley and caressed the pulsing centre of her female sexuality, his touch making her cry out, torn between her need to press herself closer to his caress and her fear of doing so because of the intensity of that need.

'This pleases me. It pleases me and it makes me want to do this...'

Alena cried out again when she felt his mouth against the place where his thumb rested.

'And this...' His fingers slid slowly and carefully into her.

It was the wildness of Alena's response, her lack of control and her desire that was affecting him and snapping the cords of his own control, Kiryl told himself. Nothing else.

Lost in the waves of pleasure that were pounding through her, each one deeper and more intense than the one before, Alena could only cling helplessly to Kiryl and plead with him, 'I want you, Kiryl, I want you now. Please now...'

The answering surge of his own flesh in its need to feel the soft warmth of her sheathing and holding it had Kiryl for the first time in his life fumbling slightly with urgency as he reached towards his discarded clothes to retrieve the condom he had brought with him. There was, after all, nothing he did not know about the way Alena lived her life—and that included the knowledge that she did not use any form of birth control. It was not, though, the urgency of his body to complete the journey that it had begun that had him tensing in the act of opening the foil packet so much as his unwanted but unignorable ache of need to be with Alena without any barriers between them—to feel her flesh around his with every intimacy there was.

This was a feeling so alien to him that it locked his breath in his throat. He never, *ever* had unprotected sex. The thought of doing so was wholly repugnant to him. It simply wasn't a risk he had ever wanted to take—and yet right here, right now, there was something… a need, a compulsion, a longing…something within him that wanted his flesh to be at one with hers, and it ripped into what he believed he knew about himself.

It was as though he had looked deep into a mirror and seen reflected there an image of all those things he had buried so deep inside himself that he had convinced himself they no longer existed.

Whatever was responsible for those feelings it had to be ignored. Kiryl knew that, but his fingers still hesitated over a task so familiar to him that it should have taken a mere breath to accomplish—instead of so long that Alena was sobbing her own need against his ear, her body shuddering with the need for the satisfaction he was denying it.

Finishing his self-appointed task, he turned towards her.

Alena was cast adrift in a new world—a world of sensation and delight and longing and love. Surely the most complete love she would ever know? Certainly the only love she would ever *want* to know. Kiryl was kissing her breasts, and then he tongued her nipples, the gentle caress a form of torture and torment when all she wanted was the immediate satisfaction of the savage clawing need he had unleashed inside her. But then his teeth again raked her nipple, causing her back to arch, and her cry of molten agonised pleasure was taken by Kiryl's kiss as he took her mouth in a deeply passionate kiss.

The slow, penetrative thrust of his tongue against hers was mirrored by the thrust of his body within her own. And how she welcomed that intimacy. How her body opened and quivered with delight and longing—how her flesh clung lovingly to his, holding it and tightening around it, her muscles moving rhythmically against each movement of his until Alena felt as though she was weightless, soaring higher and higher on the wings of her pleasure, dazzled by the brilliance and the wonder of it. Like a journey to the stars, the feeling was so magical, so perfect and so filled with pleasure, that with each increased surge of that pleasure she felt there could be no more—only to discover that there was.

She opened the eyes she had closed tightly when Kiryl had first entered her and looked up at him, her heart turning over inside her chest when she saw that he was looking back at her. How could there be any greater intimacy than this, their flesh united into one perfect whole? Everything that was in her heart was open and revealed in her gaze. She reached up to Kiryl and touched his face.

'I love you.' Her eyes widened, her body

arching as the shock of the final pleasure seized her and took her, making her hold on to Kiryl for safety and sanity.

It wasn't Alena's sobbed cry of wonderment and completion that stilled Kiryl's body in the aftershock of his release. It was his mental reaction to the intensity of the harsh cry of discovery and loss he himself had given. With its echoes still shuddering through his head he knew that it had touched something so unbearably painful inside him that it had stripped him of all his defences. It was something he could never and must never revisit. And it was Alena's fault. *She* had caused him to feel what he had no wish to feel. Something he had promised himself a long time ago he would never feel.

The plan. He must focus on that, and on his goal, and not think about that handful of seconds when—ridiculously—he had felt as though he was holding in his arms everything he had ever wanted or would ever want.

She was safe, held in Kiryl's arms, having survived the storm of desire and pleasure he had aroused within her.

Wonderingly, Alena traced the shape of Kiryl's lips with a slightly shaky fingertip. 'I'm so lucky to have met you,' she whispered. 'So very, very lucky. I love you, Kiryl. You mean everything to me.'

Something—a softening, a tenderness, a leap of hope like the flicker of light in the darkness—something as vague as the finest tendrils of early-morning mist—was happening inside him. Something so dangerous that he automatically jerked against its unwanted presence and steeled himself against it. Such feelings could only make him vulnerable—as he had been as a boy—and he had promised himself he would never be vulnerable again. Let Alena be as foolishly emotional as she wished. Those emotions could not and must not touch *him*, never mind evoke emotions of his own.

The very thought brought an inner anger against that vulnerability she had come close to causing. His voice slightly clipped, he told her the truth. 'As you do to me.'

The tone of Kiryl's voice filled Alena with renewed tenderness towards him. He was clearly embarrassed about talking about his emotions—no doubt as a result of his unhappy childhood. With her love for him she would try to find a way to ease the pain of that childhood for him, and to soften the painful memories of his father's cruel rejection of him. Love for him flooded through her.

They had three days together in St Petersburg. The most wonderful three days Alena could have imagined having, if her imagination had ever been capable of creating such happiness—which it had not. The joy and love that being with Kiryl gave her went way beyond anything that could be imagined. She woke in the morning to his touch and his kisses, and they left her floating on a cloud of sensuality.

They spent their days enjoying the city that she knew so well together, and to her delight she was able to show Kiryl treasures in it that he had not visited before. Only once was a shadow cast over the happiness of their time together, and that was one afternoon when they were walking arm in arm together in the old quarter, with its elegant architecture of a bygone age. When Kiryl paused outside one of the magnificently grand buildings to look towards it, initially Alena thought that he had simply paused to admire it. However, when she had said admiringly, 'It's a very handsome building, isn't it?' Kiryl's face clouded.

'This was where my father lived—where I came to see him after I discovered that he was my father.'

The bitterness in Kiryl's voice made Alena's heart ache for him. How lucky she had been in her own parents, who had given her so much love. She couldn't bear to think of how hurt Kiryl must have been by his father's rejection, and how he must have suffered emotionally, yearning for his father's love and being denied.

'I'm so sorry that you had to suffer like that.' she told him softly. 'But what a terrible loss your father inflicted on himself by his behaviour in rejecting you. He could have had your love—he could have had you growing up at his side—but instead, he was too blind to see what he was denying himself.'

'That was his choice,' was all Kiryl said dismissively in response.

Alena had come to recognise that, except for those brief occasions when something touched the still open wound deep within him caused by his father, he preferred not to talk about his father or his childhood.

'I've been too busy working.'

That was his response to her mock scandalised disbelief when she obligingly changed the subject and discovered that he had never visited the fabled Winter Palace or the Hermitage Museum, with its fabled art collection.

'Well, you shall visit it now,' she had told him. 'Because there is something that you need to see.'

That 'something' was the Malachite Room which, as Alena explained to Kiryl proudly when they visited it the following day, had been designed in the late 1830s by the architect Alexander Briullov for use as a formal reception room for the Empress Alexandra Fyodorovna, wife of Nicholas I.

'It replaced the original Jasper Room, which was destroyed in the fire of 1837,' Alena told Kiryl knowledgably when they stood together inside it, having joined one of the official tours allowed to view the famous building. 'The minute I saw you I thought how at home you would be in here,' she added with a smile.

Kiryl grimaced inwardly. He doubted that

his father would have agreed. *He* would have said that the last place an unwanted son with Romany blood would be at home would be a royal palace—unless of course it was in the position of the most lowly of serfs.

'It's your eyes, you see,' Alena continued, unaware of what Kiryl was thinking. 'They are exactly the same colour as the malachite columns, and when you make love to me,' she told him huskily, 'they glow with green fire, and that tells me that you want me as much as I want you. Oh, Kiryl you've made me so happy—so much happier than I ever believed possible. I wish we could stay longer in St Petersburg.'

'So do I, but we have to return to London tomorrow.'

'You have business to attend to, I suppose.' Alena pulled a small face.

'I *do* have business to attend to,' Kiryl agreed. 'But that would not stop me remaining here. No, the reason I want to return to London is because your brother will also be there, and there is something very important I need to discuss with him.'

'You mean me? Us?' Alena guessed.

Kiryl nodded his head, and the two of them stood close together whilst the other sightseers moved past them. For once the magnificence of the Malachite Room failed to command Alena's full attention and admiration.

'It is only right that I inform your brother of our relationship and my future plans for us.'

Alena felt as though her heart was melting. 'He will probably say that we are rushing things,' she warned Kiryl.

'And I will convince him of how vitally important our relationship is,' Kiryl assured her. 'Just as once we return I intend to show you how important you are to me.'

Listening to him, and much as she loved the Hermitage, all Alena wanted was the privacy of the bedroom they were sharing, and the intimacy of his possession of her body. 'Let's go back to the island,' she whispered.

The look he gave her made her heart race and her body ache deliciously in anticipatory delight.

Later, lying in his arms whilst he traced a delicate pattern of sensual pleasure over her naked body as he leaned over her in the bed, making her body quicken again even though they had already made love once since their return, Alena told him helplessly, 'I love you so much.'

'Good,' Kiryl replied, cupping the soft warmth of her breast and kissing the pulse at the base of her throat, before teasing her with nibbling little kisses that sensitised the receptive flesh of her shoulder and neck. 'That means that my plan is working.'

'What plan?' Alena demanded as she tried valiantly to remain as in control of her arousal as he obviously was of his.

'The plan to make you love me, of course,' he responded mock-seriously.

'Oh, so you *planned* to make me love you?' Alena murmured back. She was having trouble concentrating on their wordplay because of the effect Kiryl's kisses were having on her, stealing away her self-control.

'Helplessly, wholly and besottedly,' Kiryl confirmed. 'To the point where you would give yourself completely to me and deny me nothing.'

'Mmm…' was the only response Alena could manage, and even that was lost beneath the suddenly fierce male possession of

Kiryl's mouth of her own as his knee nudged her thighs apart and her body melted with eager anticipation.

CHAPTER EIGHT

As SHE stepped into the taxi, ahead of her meeting with Dolores Alvarez at the charity's headquarters, Alena could feel nervous butterflies filling her tummy. In four hours and ten minutes' time exactly Kiryl would be meeting Vasilii at the apartment, and then he would tell him about them. Kiryl had insisted that she wasn't to say anything to Vasilii about their love for one another until then. It was *his* duty and *his* pleasure to tell her half-brother of what had happened between them, he had insisted, and Alena had conceded that role to him quite willingly. It had been hard, though, not to say anything. The temptation just to speak Kiryl's name out loud for the pleasure of feeling it on her tongue and hearing it in the air was so strong—even if she only had to do so for a couple of days.

Now, though, with Vasilii back from his business negotiations, Kiryl had an appointment to see him this afternoon, and whilst she was nervous—it was important to her that the two men she loved so much got on well—she was also excited and happy. She wanted their love to be out in the open so that they could make plans. A small private wedding was what she wanted—not a fuss—and then… and then she and Kiryl would have the rest of their lives to spend together.

Alena's toes curled into the warmth of her boots at the thought of such bliss, but the ring of her mobile interrupted her happy plans. The call brought news that her morning meeting had had to be cancelled as Dolores had gone down with a winter vomiting bug and was confined to her bed.

Leaning forward, Alena instructed the cab driver to take her back to the hotel. She would while away the time whilst she waited for Kiryl to arrive in reading the latest reports from those people overseeing the charity's projects. She was still determined to convince Vasilii that she was mature enough to take over the charity now.

* * *

As she let herself into the apartment the sound of male voices came from the half-open door of the room in the apartment that her brother used as his office. That wasn't unusual—but the unexpected discovery that one of those voices belonged to Kiryl was enough to stop Alena in her tracks. The now familiar joy of knowing he was close cascaded happily through her. She had no idea what had brought Kiryl to the apartment so far ahead of his appointment with her half-brother, but her heart still sang. Perhaps he had been so impatient to be with her that he had brought his meeting with Vasilii forward, so that he could surprise her on her own return? She started to walk towards the door.

Oblivious to Alena's return, inside the room Kiryl faced Alena's half-brother as he waited to deliver his ultimatum.

He had changed his appointment with Vasilii deliberately, so that he could see him without Alena being there. That way he would be long gone before Alena got back from her meeting at the charity's offices and it would be left to her brother to tell her about the reality of Kiryl's relationship with her and its purpose.

Alena.

Kiryl was caught off-guard by the sudden jolt to his heart caused by the thought of her. That should not have happened. It had only happened because he had let it happen—because somehow he had let Alena slip into his thoughts, just as he had done last night, lying alone in bed without her, his body aching treacherously for her, dangerously aware of how empty his bed had felt without her lying within the curve of his arm, her soft breath warming his skin.

Alena—with her open and total giving of herself to him without holding back. Alena—who loved him. Love? What was that? *Nothing.* And if his bed felt empty without her—well, he would soon replace her, Kiryl told himself. She meant nothing to him as a person, after all. She was simply a pawn to be used and then discarded.

He had no emotional feelings. How could he? Emotional feelings were a weakness. From his past he heard his father's jeering laughter as he looked down at him, lying in the gutter, trying to conceal his misery.

'You are your Romany mother's child, all right. You have her foolish emotional weakness. No true son of mine would *ever* show such weakness.'

His mother's child with his mother's weaknesses. Weaknesses that had to be crushed into oblivion. Only by sharing his father's lack of emotion could he stand taller than him. And only by doing that could he fulfil the vow he had made to himself lying in that gutter.

So why was he hesitating? Why was everything he had worked for single-mindedly and for so long being threatened by his weakness now? Why was he allowing himself to even *acknowledge*, never mind listen to, whatever it was inside him that gripped him with the need to simply turn and walk away. Why was this unwanted voice inside him urging him to change his mind? Why was this weakness— his mother's weakness—interfering with his plans now? Was it because he was being tested to see if he would be tempted to weaken? If so then that temptation was a test he must endure and survive. He *must* reach his goal—if he failed then he would never be able to call himself the man the young Kiryl had promised himself he would be. The man who would succeed where the father who had despised him had failed.

And yet still he could not rid himself completely of the image inside his head of Alena looking at him, her silver-grey eyes luminous with love. He could even hear her voice breaking with the agonised joy of their sexual pleasure. If he closed his eyes he knew that he would be able to recall the feel of her touch on his skin.

Alena...

No! The denial roared silently from the damaged heart of the child he had once been. It was a sound that he could not ignore. If he did not give that child what he needed then who would? No one. There was no one—only him. Alena had her brother, and all the men who would love her and comfort her—and they *would* love her. A sharp, savage, slicing pain bit into him.

Ignoring it, he faced Alena's half-brother as they stood either side of the fireplace.

Vasilii Demidov was as tall as he was himself, although a few years older. His dark hair was cut short and his skin was warmer toned than Alena's, even though he had the same silver-grey eyes. A hand seemed to tighten around Kiryl's heart. Because after today he would never look into Alena's eyes again and see there her love for him. But that did not matter. Nothing mattered other than getting this contract—and he would sacrifice everything that had to be sacrificed in order to get it. *Everything*.

Deliberately he held Vasilii's gaze.

'I altered the time of our appointment because I wanted to speak with you without Alena being here,' Kiryl began.

Behind the door, on the point of entering the room, Alena hesitated.

Vasilii frowned slightly. 'You know my sister?' he queried.

The question seemed to hang on the air, as though it wanted to give Kiryl the time to reject it—a final chance to step back.

Ruthlessly Kiryl crushed into silence the voice inside him that was trying to make him waver from his cause.

'Yes.' Meeting Vasilii's questioning look

head-on, Kiryl told him unemotionally, 'She believes herself to be in love with me.' He paused, and then added equally unemotionally, 'In fact she believes that she and I are destined to be together, and that nothing and no one can part us.'

A burst of fire briefly darkened the silver-grey eyes. Anger? If so it was controlled quickly. The look he was now being given was one of clinical assessment.

'I see. And you, I take it, have encouraged her in this belief for reasons of your own which I imagine, from the tone of your voice, have nothing to do with you returning her feelings?'

'That is correct,' Kiryl agreed. It was good news for him that Alena's half-brother was so quick on the uptake, but knowing Vasilii's reputation in business he had not expected anything less.

Disbelief, like a single drop of icy cold water, touched Alena's senses as she stood outside the room listening to Kiryl speaking—so analytically and without a trace of emotion in his voice, as though she was a stranger to him, as though the love she had given him so freely and so passionately meant nothing to him at all. But that couldn't be possible—not after the way he had held her and touched her. It just couldn't.

'When you e-mailed me to bring the time of our appointment forward, you said that it was a business matter you wished to discuss with me,' she heard her half-brother saying.

'It is,' Kiryl agreed. 'A business matter of great importance to me.'

'A business matter that is more important than Alena's love for you?'

Vasilii's question echoed Alena's own un-spoken confusion. She held her breath whilst she waited for Kiryl's answer, praying that he would say something to explain the bewilder-ing and frightening confusion of what she had already heard him say.

'It is my good luck that Alena loves me as much as she does.'

Unsteadily Alena exhaled her pent-up breath. There had been no reason for her disquiet after all. But then, just as she would have flown into the room to Kiryl's side, he continued.

'It is, after all, Alena's unquestioning love

for me that is enabling me to put my business proposition to you.'

What was happening? What was Kiryl saying? Alena couldn't understand what was going on, and yet instinctively she felt apprehensive and fearful—as though something dark and treacherous was reaching out to hurt her love, like a dark shadow threatening to diminish the bright light of the sun. She wanted to run into the other room and demand to know what was going on, but somehow she couldn't move or even speak, condemned to simply stand there out of sight, forced to listen to what was being said.

'What kind of business proposition?'

Kiryl could hear the ominous warning note in Vasilii's voice but he ignored it. 'You and I, as I am sure you already know, are now the only two contenders for the contract to build and run the new container shipping port. As your wealth is far greater than mine, and your standing is that of a man whose antecedents had an elite standing in our community, that has to stack the odds of winning the contract more heavily in your favour than it does mine.'

'Because I have both the financial and social wherewithal to ensure that I secure the contract, you mean?' Vasilii responded.

Alena's shock intensified. Was Kiryl really suggesting that her brother would bribe officials in order to win the contract? If so he couldn't have been listening to what she had told him about her half-brother—how important honesty and anti-corruption in business dealings was to him, just as it had been to their father.

'Exactly,' Kiryl agreed. 'Which is why I decided that it would be in my own interests to tilt the playing field to my benefit. Let's not waste time. Alena believes she loves me. Nothing you can say or do will alter that. She is mine to do with as I please. She will defy any and every embargo you choose to put on whatever relationship I choose to have with her.'

Alena. Alena who looked at him with so much love in her eyes. Alena who would give him anything he asked of her. *Alena.* A woman. Just a woman. Women were weak. Their emotions made them weak. He had only to think of his own mother to know that. He would not allow any emotions to stand in his way. So why was he having to fight against the savage, angry ache inside him, that driving furious urgency that was almost an agonised yearning, biting into him and filling his senses with images of the time he had spent in St Petersburg with Alena? It threatened to undermine his resolution. It was her fault. She had made him weak, just as his father had always said he was. The useless, weak and unwanted result of giving in to a moment's sexual need.

'Alena has said nothing to me of even knowing you, never mind loving you as you claim.' Vasilii's voice was tightly controlled.

'I told her not to.' Kiryl lifted his shoulders expressively. 'You are a successful businessman who has succeeded in a very hard world. I am your competitor for this contract and you will have had me investigated, as I did you. You will know my history.'

'I know that your father was a man my father said was the most callous and corrupt man he had ever come across, and that your mother was—'

'A Romany gypsy, and as such despised by my father. Yes. That is true. He loathed the fact that I existed. My mother's blood made me unacceptable to him then just as it still makes me unacceptable to many people now. Your own bloodlines, though, are far more exalted. Your father comes from a family of the ruling elite. Your mother was a princess amongst her own people. You have the reputation of being a very proud man. Some would say a very arrogant man.'

'Some would say the same thing about you.'

'My pride and arrogance, if I have them, come from what I have achieved for myself—not what I have inherited. But that pride does not blind me to reality. You will not want to see your sister being flaunted in front of our world as my current mistress and then discarded. She is far too valuable a pawn to you for that.'

Kiryl looked towards the window. Now, when he should be consolidating his position by informing Alena's brother of just how much of herself Alena had already given to him, and with what passion and intensity, he was experiencing a strange reluctance to do so. It was as though a door had locked inside him, protecting that information—and Alena—safely behind it, as though he actually *wanted* to protect her. He simply could not say the words that would reveal the completeness with which Alena had given herself to him already.

But it seemed that her half-brother had worked things out for himself and didn't need those words, because he asked curtly, 'You and Alena are lovers?'

'I have taken her to bed, yes.'

The hard, cold, almost stilted words were meant to distance him from any voice within that might dare to remind him of just how appropriate the word 'lovers' was to describe the intimacy he and Alena had shared. Instead they felt like the blows of an axe, striking directly into him and causing indescribable pain. The last time he had felt like this had been when his father had rejected him. As he was now rejecting Alena. Why should that cause him pain?

Outside in the other room, Alena was still unable to move. How could Kiryl be doing this to her? If anyone had told her what he was saying she would have refused to believe them, she knew. But, having heard him herself, she could not. The pain was all-consuming, tearing viciously at her and threatening to destroy her completely.

Angry with himself for allowing his unwanted emotions to sidetrack him from his purpose in being here, Kiryl delivered his ultimatum.

'As yet no one other than Alena and myself—and now, of course, you—knows of our relationship. You are an intelligent man. I don't have to tell you that once she is known publicly as my mistress her value as your pawn will decrease a very great deal. However, I am prepared to renounce Alena and to walk away from her, leaving you free to arrange whatever marriage for her you ultimately decide upon, if you agree to drop out of this contract race. Furthermore, I will never speak of our relationship to anyone and no one will ever need to know that it existed.' Kiryl gave a dismissive shrug. 'We both know it will be either as a bribe or a reward that you will give her in marriage, and to the highest bidder. For that to happen her value must not be diminished—as it could be if I choose to do it.'

Alena felt as though her heart had stopped beating—as though her whole world was standing still. And then it came. The most intense emotional pain she had ever experienced. Her heart was pierced by it and filled with it. Like winter striking swiftly and cruelly deep in St Petersburg, she could feel the unbearable pain of the destruction of her dreams.

'Winning this contract is obviously very important to you,' Vasilii told Kiryl.

'It is the most important thing in my life.' As far as Kiryl was concerned there was no need for him not to make that admission. 'With this contract I shall finally create a business empire greater than my father's and do something he himself could not achieve. In doing so I shall prove myself the greater man, despite my mother's blood. I have thought of nothing else since the day he left me in the gutter outside his house.'

Kiryl knew his father had boasted about the way he had treated him quite openly, so Vasilii was bound to have heard the story. There had been plenty of occasions during his long climb to where he was now when those he had been doing business with had enjoyed reminding him of it, only realising too late their mistake when he punished them for their amusement at his expense.

And yet, incomprehensibly, the images forming inside his head now weren't of his father, or even of his triumph. Instead they were of Alena. Alena lying in his arms, looking up at him with eyes silvered with love. Alena laughing as they stood watching children playing in the snow, her arm tucked through his as she leaned into him. Alena clinging to him in the back of the troika he had hired as it raced across the snow. Alena so proud and happy when she talked about her mother's work and her own plans to build on what she had created. Alena looking from the malachite columns in the Malachite Room to his eyes, her gaze melting with love for him. Alena wanting him, and loving him, and talking of their future together.

What was happening to him? He shouldn't be thinking about her now—and most certainly not in such emotional terms. He forced himself to focus on Alena's half-brother instead.

Vasilii had walked over to the window and was standing there with his back to him.

There was no doubt in Kiryl's mind that Vasilii would accept his ultimatum, but instead of being filled with anticipatory triumph there was a feeling of flat emptiness inside him.

Alena's brother turned back to him and said evenly, 'I am prepared to withdraw from the contest between us for the contract,' he told Kiryl. 'But only if instead of giving up Alena you marry her.'

CHAPTER NINE

'Marry Alena?'

Kiryl stared at the other man, too stunned by his words to be able to conceal his shock. And yet beneath that shock his heart was leaping with such an almighty bound against his chest wall that it felt as though somehow he had suddenly and unexpectedly been thrown a rope to save him from a deep pit of darkness and loss. As though he had been offered something he had secretly ached for in the very depths of his being. As though miraculously at the last hour he had been saved from himself.

'You're saying that you want me to marry Alena?' Had he perhaps misheard or misunderstood what the other man had said? Apparently not, because Alena's half-brother was now speaking calmly.

'Yes, that is what I am saying. In the circumstances I think it would be for the best. Your agreement to a speedy marriage in return for mine not to challenge you for the contract.'

Marriage to Alena. Alena who loved him, who had given him herself and something so sweet and lost to him that....

But, no. He must not think like that. The old habit of rejecting his emotions was fighting fiercely for control inside him—reminding him, warning him, of how much he had suffered before he had learned to exclude the desire to give and receive love from his life. How much stronger he had been since doing that. How much safer, how much more free to concentrate on the really important things in life—like besting his father. It would be madness for him to weaken now and allow himself to have feelings for Alena. He could never allow himself to have that kind of emotional need for anyone. No. If his spirits had lifted at the thought of taking Alena as his wife, then it was simply because of the commercial benefits marriage to her would bring. As Vasilii Demidov's half-sister she was—as he had already told himself—a valuable asset.

Logically, and from a practical point of view, marriage to Vasilii Demidov's half-sister would be advantageous to him—but recklessly, and dangerously, there was still that feeling in a deep and complex place within him that would not go away.

It was that, Kiryl knew, that was responsible for him saying unsteadily, 'Very well,' and then taking the hand Vasilii extended to shake on their agreement.

Outside in the other room, Alena made a small agonised sound of protest and denial. This could not be happening. To listen whilst Kiryl revealed the truth about their relationship and his plans for her had been bad enough, but now to hear her beloved brother offering her to him in marriage was more than she could cope with. Vasilii couldn't mean what she had just heard him say. He couldn't.

Released from her frozen immobility, Alena rushed into the other room, oblivious to the shock her appearance caused both men.

'Alena.'

They both spoke at the same time, but it was

Kiryl's voice that was raw and ragged with emotion.

'*No*. You can't mean it, Vasilii. I *won't* marry him,' Alena burst out passionately, and all the horror she felt at what she had heard was clear in her voice as she continued, before either of them could say anything, 'I heard everything, Vasilii.' She was deliberately keeping her back to Kiryl, unable to endure the thought of looking at him. 'All of it. Every single word.'

From somewhere she managed to drag out of her pain a lifeline of anger to cling on to, to stop herself from being submerged in her own grief. Only that frail fragile thread of anger enabled her to turn towards Kiryl, pain darkening her eyes to the dark grey of stormy seas.

'You might think that you have succeeded in your plan to use me to blackmail Vasilii into letting you win the contract, but you haven't,' she told him fiercely. 'That plan depended on me loving you and…and being blind to what you really are. But I'm not blind to reality now. Now the only thing I feel for you is contempt—for you and for myself, for being stupid enough not to see you for what you really are.' Despite her best efforts, the pain of her true emotions at the cruel destruction of her dreams made Alena's voice shake slightly. 'I never want to see you again—ever.' Bravely she told him, 'I didn't love *you*. I loved someone I created inside my own head and heart—someone I now know never existed. That was weak and foolish of me. I made it easy for you to deceive me, but I shall never make that mistake again. And as for marrying you. I'd rather stay single all my life.'

'I'm sorry, Alena, but I'm afraid that you *must* marry him.'

Alena stared up at her brother.

'What? Vasilii, you can't mean that. I know what he is now. He doesn't have the power to force you to give up the contract because he doesn't have *me* any more.'

'The situation isn't as simple or as clear-cut as that. I'm afraid there is no other choice for you, Alena. Not if what I have been told about the intimacy of your relationship is true.' Vasilii paused before continuing, 'Of course, if it is not…'

Vasilii meant if they had not been lovers. Alena's heart sank. If only she could be more like Kiryl and lie without any compunction. But she wasn't and she couldn't.

As the reality of what Vasilii had said started to sink in, involuntary tremors of distress and misery shook her body. To her shock she saw that Kiryl had taken a step towards her. Immediately and instinctively she stepped back. She couldn't let him touch her. She couldn't. Because even after what she had heard she was still afraid that if he did touch her he might find some rebellious cell within her body that would defy her and respond to him. No, of course not. That would *never* happen now. No, she was stepping back because the thought of him touching her revolted her—nothing else.

But as she struggled to come to terms with what was happening, her half-brother's grim words had her switching her attention to him with growing disbelief. 'You might not see it that way at the moment, but by brokering a deal that includes marriage to Kiryl for you I am trying to protect you and our family's good name.'

She shook her head, pleading with him in an anguished voice, '*No*, Vasilii.'

''I'm sorry, Alena, but you must marry him.

However, the marriage need not last long,' Vasilii told her. 'If it helps, try to think of it as a coat that will give you the protection of respectability when you most need it.'

Was that supposed to reassure her? Marriage to Kiryl would be more like a shroud wrapped so tightly around her self-respect that it would destroy it.

'Vasilii, please,' she pleaded.

'Believe me, you will find it much easier to live your future life as a respectable divorcee than as a discarded mistress. We are all judged by our circumstances, no matter how little we may like that fact. We are accorded or denied respect according to how others judge us. I would not like to see you become the kind of woman who is passed from man to man for pleasure before being discarded—and that is what I fear could happen.'

'I would never let that happen to me,' Alena protested, fresh shock filling her as she listened to her half-brother's unvarnished home-truths.

'You might not have any choice. Should Kiryl choose to make the details of your relationship public, then you will automatically be judged by other men to be equally available to them. As your husband, though, it will be his duty to protect your reputation as his wife. This is a business arrangement—a bargain in which we all lose something just as we all gain something—and it is as necessary for the honour of our family name as it is for Kiryl's desire to win the contract. If you had told me before getting involved with him things might have been different, of course. But since you did not...'

It was all her own fault. That was what Vasilii was saying to her. And deep down inside herself Alena knew that she agreed with him. If she hadn't created that silly fantasy inside her head about Kiryl then perhaps she would have thought more logically and carefully about his motives when he had actually approached her. And what about when he had taken her to bed? Would she have been capable of thinking logically about his motives then?

How easy he must have found it to make use of her own vulnerability to him. She had been so naïve, thinking that he wanted her as much as she had wanted him, that his feelings for her were the same as hers for him. He had been able to dupe and deceive her because she had *wanted* to believe him. And now she must pay for that lack of judgement.

Had their father still been alive things might have been different. He had often gently teased Vasilii about the traditional paternalistic ideas he had absorbed from the time he had spent with his maternal grandparents after the death of his mother. The fusion of Arab and nomad blood within his mother's tribe meant that, for all he was a twenty-first-century citizen of the world, her half-brother could be rather old-fashioned when it came to certain moral issues. She had never imagined, though, that it would ever impact on her own life in the way it was doing now.

'Kiryl and I have already shaken hands on our agreement,' Vasilii told her. 'Your marriage to him will take place as soon as it can be arranged.'

'But not until Kiryl has secured the contract,' Alena couldn't resist putting in, her voice brittle with all that she was feeling as she looked directly at Kiryl for the first time. 'After all, that *is* what all this is about for you, isn't it, Kiryl? This is what it has all been about for you right from the start.'

She was trembling from head to foot, Kiryl could see, her emotions spilling past her self-control and into her voice so that he could hear her pain. Pain where such a short time ago there had been joy and happiness. *He* was responsible for that pain.

Something unfamiliar and previously unknown was growing into life inside him. Remorse? Guilt? Kiryl didn't know. He only knew that it made him want to reach out to Alena, to hold her and comfort her, to tell her that it wasn't too late for him to stop things. He could pull out of the deal—tell Vasilii that he had changed his mind.

What? What on earth was happening to him? He couldn't really be thinking about throwing away everything he had worked so hard for and risk losing the contract that was so vitally important to him just because of Alena's pain. She meant nothing to him, and that was the way he wanted things to stay.

'This marriage is for the best, Alena. I promise you that.'

'The best for whom?' Alena challenged her brother bleakly. 'Certainly not for me.'

Was that a sigh she could hear from Vasilii? Hardly. She was just imagining it—just as she had imagined that look of torment she thought she had seen briefly in Kiryl's eyes.

'You are both as bad as one another,' she told them tonelessly. 'Two businessmen for whom I am simply a bargaining tool, like a slave to be bought and sold to suit your purposes.'

She couldn't bear what was happening. She really couldn't. Unable to trust herself to say any more, she turned and fled to the sanctuary of her own bedroom, locking the door behind her.

She might feel that she couldn't bear the situation she was now in, but Alena knew that she would have to. She had no other choice. Financially she was totally dependent on Vasilii. She had nothing of her own other than what was in her bank account and a wardrobe full of clothes. She had no training she could fall back on, no qualifications, and she knew her half-brother well enough to know that, having made up his mind about her future, he would not change it. If she tried to escape her unwanted marriage he would track her down and find her. The only solace she had was what Vasilii had said to her about the marriage only needing to be of short duration.

Standing alone in her bedroom, looking out of the window onto the windswept London rooftops below her, Alena made herself a promise.

The two men she had trusted absolutely, whom she had thought loved her as much as she loved them, had betrayed her cruelly and callously, destroying not just her belief in them but her ability to trust and her belief in love itself—at least for her. Some people like her mother, her parents, were lucky—they found true love. But she was obviously not one of them. Not worthy of being loved. Only worthy of being used.

She pushed that thought away. She might have to marry Kiryl, but hopefully her sentence would be a short one and then she would be free. And from the searing pain of what she had endured Alena vowed that a new Alena would be created, rising from the ashes of what she had once been like the legendary phoenix, to be stronger, better, wiser—an Alena who would never again allow anyone to hurt her. This new Alena would control her own life and make her own choices, and those choices and decisions would not include allowing any other man into her life to hurt her as both Kiryl and Vasilii had. She would use the time during which she was forced to be married to Kiryl to forge her own future. And that future would be her mother's charity. Her future and the focus of her life.

A new sense of purpose filled her, and with it a steely strength. Her reward for agreeing to this marriage that Vasilii was insisting upon would be the right to control the charity. Kiryl and her brother would have to learn that they were not the only ones who could issue ultimatums and strike bargains.

Kiryl. The pain she had been holding at bay ever since she had realised the truth about him surged through her, making her want to cry out in agony against its savaging of her emotions. But Alena wasn't going to give in to that raking clawing pain. It must be endured, suffered—because that was what would make her stronger.

CHAPTER TEN

WEDDING dresses. Alena was trying her best to avoid looking at them, but it was next to impossible when she was surrounded by them as she sat in the salon of an exclusive upmarket wedding dress designer whilst a variety of models paraded dresses in front of her for inspection. It had been Vasilii, of course, who had made the appointment for her. *She* couldn't care less what she wore for a wedding she didn't want to a man who didn't want her and had never wanted her—even if he had pretended otherwise. She'd rather wear sackcloth and ashes.

Her throat went tight as she fought against the upsurge of misery that threatened her. It wasn't because of any treacherous feelings for Kiryl that she was feeling like this. He meant nothing to her now—less than nothing. No, it was the sight of all those white dresses, with their symbolism of happiness and hope, so outdated in modern-day society with their fragile delicacy, their sheer impracticability, their inability to withstand the reality of a world that would trample on them. Rather like marriage itself. Entered into with such dreams and hopes. But not for her. Her marriage would not be like that.

As she had come into the showroom two other women had been leaving, mother and daughter by the look of them, their shared happiness in the smiles they exchanged reminding Alena of all that she had lost with the death of her own mother. Her mother would never have let this happen to her. *Her mother.* Alena closed her eyes and blinked against the dryness of a pain that went too deep for tears.

She would have to choose something, of course. There was no point in drawing out this senseless parody of what choosing her wedding dress should be. The model standing in front of her now was wearing a gown so beautiful that the sight of it should have filled her heart with delight. Had she been a true bride-to-be, about to marry the man she loved, then this would be the dress she would have chosen, Alena recognised. The slender column of silk-satin was cut and seamed so that it fell elegantly to the floor after gently caressing the model's body, its neckline and arms covered by the most delicate lace that Alena had ever seen. Tiny crystal bugle beads sewn into the seams at the back of the dress to form a train gave just the right amount of shimmer. It was the kind of wedding dress she would have loved to have worn for Kiryl had he been the man she'd originally thought him.

The sight of the dress, so beautiful, representing that special something of a love that should be pure filled her with more pain. She couldn't bear to be there any more. She couldn't bear to think of wearing one of these beautiful gowns at a ceremony that would be meaningless for a marriage that would be devoid of all the things marriage should be. She didn't care what she wore.

Abruptly she stood up, her action bringing the hovering saleswoman swiftly to her side.

'I have to go,' she told her shakily.

'But your gown—you haven't chosen anything.'

'You choose,' Alena told her. 'I can't.'

'But you'll need to try the dress on,' the saleswoman protested.

Alena shook her head.

'No. Just choose something for me and then have it altered and sent to the apartment, please.'

They had her measurements. They'd measured her when she arrived. The last thing she felt like doing now was standing in front of a mirror looking at a reflection of herself in a dress for a wedding she didn't want.

All the other arrangements had now been made. Their engagement had been announced within hours of the deal made by Kiryl and Vasilii, and now their June wedding was less than three weeks away. Not that Alena had been involved with the plans for the ceremony. Over the weeks that had passed since their engagement she had flatly refused to have anything whatsoever to do with it, leaving the two men she now thought of as her betrayers to make what arrangements they chose. They were to be married in a civil ceremony in St Petersburg, followed by a lavish wedding party—and that was the final callous treachery as far as Alena was concerned. That she should be forced to 'celebrate' a travesty of everything she had hoped her marriage would be in the city that meant so much to her, where she had believed she had found a love as perfect as the one shared by her parents.

Her only solace in the humiliation and misery she was being forced to endure was her involvement with the charity. Vasilii had not been inclined to agree to her demand to be allowed to take control of it initially, when she had returned to his office to confront him with her demand, but Kiryl had stepped in, his expression shuttered and his voice devoid of emotion as he spoke to her brother.

'I would prefer it if you would agree. It will give her something to do whilst I am away on business.'

For a minute she had been tempted to say that she had changed her mind, that simply by speaking as he had Kiryl had contaminated the charity, just as he had contaminated what she had thought of as their love. But then the new cool and clinical Alena she had become reminded her that the charity would ultimately be her escape route to a freedom in which she'd control her own life, so she had bitten back her rejection and Vasilii had nodded his head and given way.

After her morning spent looking at wedding dresses she didn't want to wear, the last thing Alena felt like doing was going to view the townhouse in exclusive Knightsbridge that Kiryl had arranged for them to rent for the brief duration of their marriage. Alena didn't care where they lived. All she cared about was getting back her self-respect, and that could never happen whilst she was married to Kiryl. Kiryl, however, had insisted that it was necessary for her to give approval to the house he had chosen, and Vasilii had backed him up.

Before she had realised the truth about Kiryl she would have been thrilled at the thought of living *anywhere* with him, never mind this smart townhouse, Alena admitted as she got out of a taxi outside the address Kiryl had given her. The house was Georgian in style, in a pretty leafy square with its own private garden.

Climbing the steps, Alena rang the bell to one side of the highly glossed black-painted door. To her dismay it was Kiryl, not the estate agent she had assumed would be there, who opened the door for her.

Automatically she stepped back, flinching when Kiryl reached out and took hold of her arm to draw her into the hallway of the house, with its immaculate off-white-painted walls and its wrought-iron staircase that curled elegantly upwards.

'Why are you here?' Alena demanded, pulling herself free of Kiryl's hold. 'After all there's no one here to see us acting out this... this appalling charade.'

'Perhaps I wanted to make sure that the house is to your liking,' Kiryl responded in a terse voice, before telling her curtly, 'I suggest that we start upstairs and then work our way down. If there's anything you don't like, please let me know. I've taken the house fully furnished, but obviously if you wish to change anything—'

'There's only one thing I want to change, and that's the fact that I ever met you,' Alena told him bitterly, heading for the stairs.

The house had obviously been handed over to a top interior designer to work on. On the uppermost floor were a guest suite and two smaller bedrooms sharing a bathroom. From the window of one of them she could see down into the private garden in the square. Two young women were sitting on a bench there, buggies parked close to them.

Children. Alena's heart ached as though someone was tearing it apart.

'Are you happy with these rooms?' Kiryl asked.

Although she had her back to him, Alena could feel him standing behind her. If she turned round she would be so close to him that all it would take for her to be in his arms was one single small step. In his arms. That was the last thing she wanted. The security she had thought was there for her with him had never been anything more than a lie—just like everything else about him.

'Am I really supposed to believe that you care what I think?' she challenged.

Down in the garden, one of the women lifted a small child out of its buggy. Alena had to turn away to escape from that emotive sight. Once—a lifetime ago now—she had actually dreamed of having Kiryl's children. Children to whom they could both give the love Kiryl himself had been denied as a child. How deluded she had been. Delighted, deluded and deceived. Blindly, Alena headed for the stairs.

In the square hallway at their foot, Kiryl opened one of the doors, telling her, 'This is the master bedroom suite.'

Unwillingly Alena stepped past him and into the room. Large and rectangular, it was decorated in the same off-white colour scheme, broken up by the rich colour of the dark grey silk curtains and the wallpaper behind the bed. Like the room upstairs she had just left, it too looked down onto the square's garden.

The buggies and the women were still there. The pain in her heart felt like a volcano about to erupt, but Alena knew that she had to force her emotions back down inside herself—at least for the duration of this hated, unwanted and humiliating marriage.

She didn't realise that Kiryl had come to stand at her side until she heard him ask, 'What are you looking at?'

Moving away from him, she told him in a brittle voice, 'The children. At least I'm to be spared the horror of having your child, Kiryl. I couldn't bear to think I'd brought a child into the world who might grow up like *you*. Do you know that when you first told me about your father I was actually stupid enough to think that what you'd experienced at his hands would make you a wonderful father? I thought you'd want to be so different to him. Because you'd never want to be considered anything like him, I thought you'd want to be the kind of father—the kind of man—who understood his children's need for his love. But I was wrong—just as I was wrong to tell myself that your father's treatment of your mother must have given you compassion and understanding for someone who loved you.

'When I thought about the boy you had been I wanted to hold that child and protect him. I wanted to tell him that it was his father who was despicable and unworthy, not him. I wanted to tell him to be proud of his mother and of himself. And when I thought of the man I believed you were I wanted to give him everything I had to give—all my love, all my loyalty, all my happiness. Everything.

'But of course you weren't that man, were you, Kiryl? You never wanted to turn your back on everything your father had been

and become a man as different from him as
it was possible to be. You never wanted to
reject everything he represented. I assumed
that was what you wanted—but it wasn't, was
it? You're just like him. There are other ways
you could have chosen to prove yourself better
than him—many other ways—but you chose
to mirror him, to *be* him—only more so.

'You were never the man I thought you
were, and I was a fool to imagine that you
could ever be. You decided to deny yourself
the opportunity to be that man a long time
ago, when you lay in the gutter watching your
father walk away. I should hate you, but instead I pity you—because no matter what you
do, or how much you succeed, you will never
know what it means to love someone, or to be
truly loved by them. Because you don't have
it in you to allow that to happen. Is this what
your mother would have wanted for you? Is
this the way she would want you to represent
the love she had for you?'

Abruptly Alena stopped speaking. She had
never intended to say all she had, and now she
felt slightly light-headed and dizzy.

She looked round the master bedroom and

then said to Kiryl emotionlessly, 'I don't know why you've insisted on me seeing this house. Wherever I have to live for the duration of this wretched marriage will feel like a prison to me. But there's one thing for certain: I might have to marry you, Kiryl, but it will be a marriage without love and without intimacy. Whichever room I sleep in I shall be sleeping in it alone. There is nothing you could do now that would ever make me desire you again.'

'Be careful when you challenge me, Alena,' Kiryl warned her angrily. Her words had pierced the armour of his self-control even though he was not going to allow her to see that. What she had said about him had ripped and opened up scar tissue he had thought hardened to withstand anything life could throw at it, but he had now discovered it was still unbearably raw.

'It isn't a challenge. It's a statement of fact,' Alena told him fiercely.

'That I can no longer make you want me? That's a fact, is it? Are you sure about that?'

Of course she was. So why was she looking anxiously to the door as Kiryl came towards her? He penned her in between the window and his body, a male gleam in his eyes that warned Alena that she had gone too far. But what she had said to him was true, wasn't it? There wasn't anything he could do now that would arouse her desire. After all that desire had been for the man she had believed him to be—not the man she had discovered he was.

'Hunger for another person's touch isn't something you can turn on and off. It isn't something you can control or subjugate to your own will.' As he had already discovered, Kiryl acknowledged, remembering night upon night during which he had lain awake, his body aching for the intimacy they had shared as lovers.

Oh, yes, he might have pretended to himself that that wasn't the case. He might have denied to himself that he wanted her. But deep inside that part of himself that she had somehow managed to touch had refused to bow to his commands to accept the lie he had been telling it. It wanted her. It wanted her beyond logic or reason. It ached and hungered for her just as it was doing now.

He could see the way in which his deliberately spoken words caused Alena's eyes to darken, and his heart thudded violently into his chest wall. He had known the minute he had walked into this room and seen the dark grey curtains and the silk throw on the bed that so closely matched the colour of Alena's eyes when she was aroused that this was the house he would rent, Kiryl admitted to himself now. This was the first time he had been alone with her since the announcement of their engagement, and the scent of her as they walked from room to room together had already been maddening his senses well before she had challenged him.

'Alena...'

The familiar warmth of Kiryl's breath against her skin made Alena shudder. With rejection, not desire, she told herself. But it was a strange rejection that had her allowing him to take her in his arms and mould her body to his, and an even stranger one that had her head tilting so that he could brush her hair back from her face and then cup it whilst he looked down into her eyes before brushing her lips with his.

Such a tender, gentle kiss—and one that she could have avoided or denied instead of making that small keening sound deep in her throat. But she had made it, and Kiryl's response was to crush her even closer, kiss her deeply and intimately. Now she tried to resist him, realising the danger she was in—not from Kiryl, but from herself, in the response within her that was rising up inside her like a rip tide.

No matter how hard she tried to force her body to deny that it wanted him, the need he aroused refused to be controlled. Just the merest touch of his breath against her skin was enough to make her shudder with need, and right now Kiryl was doing far more than merely breathing against her skin. Right now Kiryl was kissing her, touching her with something that if she hadn't known better she would have believed was a savagely hungry need of his own.

His hand had found and cupped her breast, his thumb and finger caressing her nipple through her clothes. Fierce longing exploded inside her, depriving her of the ability to think or assess. When Kiryl pulled aside her clothes to lift her breast from her bra and suckle sensuously on her nipple Alena was lost. She was vaguely aware of raking his back with her nails through the fabric of his shirt, and then sobbing with a mixture of release and impatience when he pressed her lower body into his, his hand on her bottom encouraging her to move her hips rhythmically against him in response to the hard presence of his erection.

He was lost—helpless—possessed by the intensity of his need for Alena, Kiryl recognised even as he tried to hold back the ferocity of need claiming him. She was all he wanted, all he would ever want. He wanted to lose himself in her and let everything else fall away. All he wanted was Alena.

All he wanted? That couldn't be possible. It must not be possible. Abruptly he released her.

Shocked out of the her own desire back into reality, Alena pulled away with a small shocked cry of denial, darting past Kiryl and pausing only to pick up her handbag before running down the stairs and out into the square. Her heart was pounding. She felt physically sick with self-disgust, unable to believe what she had done and how she had felt. The sight of a cruising taxi had her flagging it down and climbing into it. And then, even with all that had happened, she was unable to stop herself from looking up towards the bedroom she had just left.

Kiryl was standing there in the window, looking down into the street. Her heart rocked to a standstill inside her chest. What had happened was all her own fault. She should never have challenged him like that. She might have guessed, knowing now the kind of man he was, that he would think nothing of adding to her humiliation by making her want him again.

And she *had* wanted him. Oh, how that knowledge scorched her pride. How could she still want him? How *could* she?

From the window Kiryl watched as the taxi bore Alena away. Thank heavens she had gone. Another handful of seconds and he would not have been able to stop himself from begging her to let him love her. *Love* her? Possess her was what he meant. That was all. She'd got him so that he couldn't think straight now. Why…? Why did she affect him the way she did? How was it possible, after all he had taught himself, for her to get under his skin and into his senses into his heart and—

His heart? Kiryl could hear the sound of his own blood drumming in his ears.

Alena.

Why was it that just thinking her name filled him with such intense longing that it felt like a form of torture?

CHAPTER ELEVEN

IN HER bedroom in the luxurious St Petersburg apartment Vasilii was renting, Alena felt the morning sunshine warming her skin through the windows from which the maid had pulled back the curtains when she had come in earlier. Warming her skin…but not as Kiryl's touch had warmed it. Nothing and no one would ever touch her in that way again. Just as nothing could or would ever take away the ache inside her for him.

Why had this had to happen to *her*? Why was she condemned to love him even though she knew he was not worthy of that love? Because she did still love him. Nothing she could say to herself seemed to stop her from doing that. A small gasp of despair escaped her. How on earth was she going to get through the mockery of their marriage without betraying her feelings? How was she going to be able to endure living under the same roof as Kiryl, knowing that he was so close to her, knowing how much she wanted him, and yet at the same time knowing that she must never allow him to see how she felt about him?

For her, Kiryl was as dangerous as any drug craved by an addict. Those moments in his arms at the house he was renting for them in London had ripped the comforting protection of her self-delusion from her eyes and revealed the truth to her, and now there was no going back from that truth. Despite everything she knew about Kiryl that should have killed her love for him; that love was still alive inside her. How that knowledge shamed and humiliated her, scorching and scalding her pride and withering her self-respect. She had thought she had touched the nadir of self-contempt in knowing that she had been so easily deceived by him, but that had been nothing compared with the way she felt about herself now for still loving him.

Her wedding dress had been delivered to the London apartment the day before they had left for St Petersburg. Alena had refused to unpack it, never mind look at it or try it on, but the maid who had come with the apartment Vasilii was renting had taken it upon herself to unpack the gown, along with the rest of Alena's things, and had been in the process of hanging it up when Alena had walked into her dressing room.

The shock of recognising that the dress the saleswoman had chosen for her was the one she herself would have loved to wear as a real bride—a bride who was loved and who loved in return—had held Alena rigidly still as she'd stared at it. Then she had started to tremble, and she suspected that had the maid not been there she would have grabbed the dress and bundled it up into as small a ball as she could before putting it somewhere she no longer needed to see it. But the maid *had* been there, and the dress had been carefully hung up in the wardrobe, the vision it represented of all that her own wedding day would not be ready to torment Alena every time she opened the wardrobe doors.

She couldn't bear to think of wearing such a perfect wedding dress for Kiryl, but she would have to. It was too late to regret now that she had not stayed at the designer's showroom and deliberately chosen the worst dress she could find. An ugly dress for a wedding that represented everything that was ugly about a marriage entered into for the reasons she and Kiryl were entering into theirs.

Staying here in bed wouldn't do her any good, Alena told herself now. Her dreams last night had been tormented by memories of how it had felt to lie in Kiryl's arms and believe that she was loved. Better to get up and face reality. And that reality was that this was surely the worst time there could be for her to be here in St Petersburg, feeling the way she did.

Summer in St Petersburg, was the season for celebrations—a time when it never truly went dark, traditionally known as 'White Nights'— the Belye Nochi, as the Russians called them. A time when all-night parties were given all over the city and especially on the islands of its delta. A time of joy in celebrating the return to warmth from the icy grip of winter. The time of St Petersburg's marriage season.

Everywhere she looked, or so it seemed to Alena, happy, loved-up brides and their grooms were posing for photographs against the backdrop of the city's elegant buildings or on its many bridges over its network of canals. In the past Alena had loved visiting St Petersburg in the summer almost as much as visiting it in the winter, but not *this* summer. Every time she saw a bride posing in her white dress, laughing lovingly up at her groom, her own heart ached even more for all that she would never have. After only two days in the city that ache had become unbearable.

Since their arrival in the city they had all been caught up in a whirl of social activities ahead of the wedding, which was to take place in three days' time. Last night the three of them had attended the exclusive and prestigious Stars of the White Nights Festival at the Mariinsky Theatre—an event which was the highlight of the city's cultural calendar, for which tickets were highly sought-after.

Formal dress was the order of the day for the event, and Vasilii had commented, as she had stood with him and Kiryl, upon how much he regretted having forgotten to arrange for her mother's jewellery to be removed from the London bank vault where it was kept so that she could wear it whilst they were in the city.

'My mother never wanted to be judged or valued as a person by the quality of her diamonds, Vasilii,' Alena had reminded him. 'And neither do I.' No amount of jewellery, however splendid, could compensate her for the emotional pain she was having to endure.

Tonight they were all attending yet another party—this one just outside St Petersburg, at a luxurious new villa built there by one of Russia's wealthiest men to celebrate his marriage earlier in the year—his third—to a well-known American actress. The festivities were to include the live appearance of a world famous pop singer, and would conclude with a firework display. The entire event was reputed to be costing millions.

Alena had no appetite either for celebrating or seeing so much money spent so lavishly. Just a tithe of that money given to charity, as her mother had always insisted that her father did, would have done so much for so many people. She hadn't even bought a new dress for the event. Instead she had brought with her from London one she already had, although she suspected that its understated elegance would probably seem dull compared with the fashions favoured by some of Russia's wealthiest socialite wives. Not that she cared. Even though Kiryl would see her wearing it.

Her heart gave an unwanted lurch inside her chest. Why did she feel like this about him when she knew that loving him could only hurt her?

A few minutes later, after she had composed herself, she walked into the main salon of the apartment and was surprised to see Vasilii sitting there, reading the London papers which he had sent to him every morning. He'd had so many business appointments that she had hardly seen him since they had arrived.

'Ah, Alena,' he greeted her, putting down his paper to stand up and come over to kiss her briefly on the cheek.

They had had such a good relationship before Kiryl, but now she felt so betrayed by the stance he had taken that Alena felt she had lost the brother she'd thought she knew.

As he wasn't a man given to open displays of affection, it surprised her when instead of releasing her he kept his arm around her, his voice unexpectedly gruff as he told her, 'I know you don't think so right now, but I promise you, Lena, that I am acting in your best interests. And if you will just trust me you will discover that for yourself.'

His use of his old pet name for her brought a lump to Alena's throat. Maybe Vasilii *did* think he was acting in her best interests, but he didn't know what she knew. He didn't know that she still loved Kiryl, and that loving someone for whom she knew she should only feel contempt was tearing her apart.

'I've got some news for you,' Vasilii continued. 'Although it won't be announced officially yet, it's been confirmed that Kiryl has won the contract. I had a telephone call from the head of the company this morning to tell me. By now I expect Kiryl will have heard the good news himself.'

Alena pulled away from her brother's hold.

'You might call it good news, Vasilii,' she told him, 'but for me it's the worst possible news there could be.'

She saw her brother shake his head, as though impatient with her words, but what she had said was the truth as far as she was concerned. Now, with his goal achieved, Kiryl would be fully turned into a man just like his father. She was in love with a man who simply did not exist—an image she had created inside her own head—and surely knowing that should have made it easy for her to cease loving him?

It had been a real man, though, who had touched her flesh and brought her body into singing, longing life. The real Kiryl who had kissed her and caressed her, taken and possessed her, until her senses and her body were totally in thrall to him—then, now and for ever, Alena admitted helplessly.

In the sitting room of his St Petersburg hotel suite Kiryl stared unseeingly at the painting on the wall above the desk where he was seated.

He had won the contract.

Where was the triumph? The sense of achievement and pleasure in having finally reached his goal and bested his father?

Where was the euphoria of victory? The sensation of standing over the fallen body of his enemy, slain by his own superiority?

Why couldn't he even manage to summon up the mental image of his father standing over him so contemptuously, as he had done so many times over the years, to increase the burn of his bitterness and to fuel his own private hunger to inflict his chosen punishment on his parent?

Why, instead of that image, was the only one that filled his senses one of Alena? Alena lying in his bed, her hair spread around her, her eyes warm and liquid with her love for him. Alena crying out in shocked pleasure as he taught her all that pleasure was. Alena holding him safe when he succumbed to his own need and his own release from it.

Alena.

He hadn't had a full night's sleep since she'd walked out on him at the house in London. He'd been angry then—angry with himself for wanting her so much that he'd broken all the rules he'd ever made for himself and then some by allowing his aching need for her to overwhelm his will power. A need that only she had aroused in him, and a need which he suspected only she would ever be able to arouse in him. He had wanted to make her desire him because of his own desire for her, but his success had backfired on him—because in gaining her response he had lost his own ability to control his reaction to her.

Acknowledging that had made him very angry with himself. He had, after all, far more important things to think about than his inconvenient and unwanted physical vulnerability to Alena.

Only he also had to acknowledge that he wasn't just physically vulnerable to her. He was emotionally vulnerable to her as well. As he'd held her in his arms before she had run away from him, what he had most wanted to hear her say wasn't that she wanted him but that she loved him.

Pacing the floor of his bedroom later that night, he had felt all the things she had said to him earlier in the day about his father and about himself come back to him. There hadn't been a day since then—or a night, and the nights were the worst—when he hadn't examined her words over and over again.

And now, when everything he had worked for was finally in his grasp, when he had achieved the goal he had worked so hard towards for so long, Kiryl felt that in reality he had nothing of any true value.

'Is this what your mother would have wanted for you?' Alena had asked. 'Is this the way she would want you to represent the love she had for you?'

For years he had deliberately stopped himself from thinking about his mother. Her pain, her humiliation at the hands of his father, had diminished her—and would diminish him if he allowed himself to recognise it. That was what he had told himself. Instead of being proud of her he had allowed his father to make him feel ashamed of her. All these years when he had thought he was being strong.

Rubbing eyes that were dry from lack of sleep, Kiryl pushed his hand into his hair and then grimaced. Vasilii had phoned him earlier, to congratulate him on winning the contract. This evening he would be escorting Alena to what would be one of the major social events of the season. There would be plenty of people there willing to congratulate him on getting the contract, and many of them would remember his father and how he had rejected him. The thought of the sweetness of that triumph had been the lodestar that had enabled him to work so tirelessly to overcome all the obstacles and the hardships he had faced. With the contract secured—and through his marriage to Alena his connection to Vasilii secured—he would have everything he had believed he would ever want.

Everything but Alena's love—that infinitely precious gift he had valued so little and then discarded, and for which he now hungered so much.

Kiryl closed his eyes against the burning ache of his own emotions and then opened then again. He had things he had to do—and do now.

Alena was just on the point of going to her room to get changed for the evening's event when a courier arrived from the St Petersburg branch of one of the world's most famous jewellery houses. The maid who had answered the door to his knock was looking far more excited than Alena felt when she brought her a discreetly monogrammed carrier bag containing beautifully gift-wrapped boxes—four of them in all.

Taking them to her room to unwrap and open them, Alena thought ruefully that her half-brother had obviously decided she *had* to have jewellery to wear tonight, even if he had to buy her some so that she could do so.

Perhaps another woman's heart would have lifted at the thought of new jewellery, but nothing could lift *her* heart, Alena knew. However, when she opened the first and largest of the leather boxes she had to admit that the beauty of the necklace inside it did make her catch her breath. In fact Alena didn't think she had ever seen something so exquisitely lovely and elegant, each diamond so pure that the light reflecting from it made her blink. Completely the opposite of ostentatious, this piece of jewellery was deliberately simple and understated, and designed by a master craftsman.

For a moment a tremulous smile touched her mouth. Vasilii obviously understood her far better than she had realised to have given her this. Everything about it said that he knew the way she thought and, more importantly, the way she felt. There was even a small note inside the box, confirming that the diamonds were ethically sourced.

Inside the other boxes were a pair of bracelets to match the necklace, and delicate drop earrings in the final box completed the set.

It had been thoughtful of Vasilii to take time out of his busy schedule to choose such a lovely gift for her, but the only gift she really wanted from her brother was to be freed from a marriage which she knew would destroy her, Alena thought with a heavy heart. How could she live side by side with Kiryl, day after day, knowing she loved him, knowing he would never return that love, and worst of all knowing what he could have been but had chosen not to be?

The silk evening dress she was wearing was a soft shade of lilac, its silk swathed and draped by its designer so that it hinted at the curves of her body rather than deliberately outlining them. High-necked and long-sleeved, the dress was semi-sheer almost to the waist at the back, and, whilst it was discreetly sensual rather than deliberately provocative, Alena was still glad that it had a matching wrap to go with it, should she feel that it was more revealing than she felt comfortable with.

In order to show off her new earrings to advantage she'd put her hair up, securing it with a pair of antique silver combs that had been one of her father's gifts to her mother. She'd finished the outfit with a pair of silver high heeled sandals and a matching silver clutch bag.

She had just spritzed her favourite scent into the air and walked into it, so that it would create a delicate cloud of scent around her as she moved, when after a brief rap on her door Vasilii opened it and walked in, dressed in the formality of a dinner suit and looking extremely handsome if somewhat formidable. Her half-brother was a very good-looking man, Alena thought ruefully. But he was also one whose autocratic manner often meant that others held him in some awe.

'Kiryl should be here any minute,' he warned her, looking at the gold dress watch he was wearing, which had originally belonged to his father. Autocratic Vasilii might be, but Alena had never doubted his love for his father. 'I suggested that the three of us should travel to the villa together.'

Alena nodded her head. Just the sound of Kiryl's name made her heart ache with pain.

'Thank you for these,' she told Vasilii, touching her new necklace and then the bracelets. 'They are absolutely beautiful, Vasilii, but you really should not have.'

'I didn't,' he responded promptly.

Alena stared at him, confusion and dismay filling her.

'Oh, no! You mean that they must have been intended for someone else.'

'I shouldn't think so. I am sure they were intended for you, Alena. But I am not the one who chose them for you. I rather think that instead they are a gift from your future husband. Something to commemorate his success, perhaps?'

Whilst Alena just looked at him the maid came in, to tell them that Kiryl had arrived and was waiting for them in the apartment's sitting room. It was too late now for her to wish she had never worn the diamonds, which now felt like a cold, mocking weight against her skin, shackling her to him. It was a bond she wanted to reject, but couldn't—just as she couldn't reject or escape her love for Kiryl himself.

* * *

The sight of Alena wearing the diamond jewellery he had chosen so carefully for her made Kiryl's heart turn over inside his chest in a blend of pain and pleasure. She looked thinner, her cheekbones more pronounced, the luminous glow gone from her eyes, but she was still incredibly beautiful A beautiful woman both inside and out, he acknowledged helplessly. He ached so badly for what he had lost, and the right it would have given him to go to her and take her in his arms.

As it was, they left the apartment and got into the limousine that was to take them to the party without Alena so much as looking at him, never mind speaking to him. What had he expected? Alena had made it plain enough to him how she felt about him and their marriage, hadn't she?

She would have to thank Kiryl for his gift and congratulate him on his success in winning the contract at some stage during the evening, Alena knew. Good manners necessitated that, she admitted. She stared out of the darkened window of their transport, leaving Vasilii and Kiryl to talk to one another in low voices, no doubt about business matters, as they were driven out of St Petersburg to the south of the city where their host had built his new villa on similar lines to those of one of St Petersburg's most famous royal palaces, although on a smaller scale.

Alena sighed a little when they approached it and turned into a long drive. Both the drive and the house were illuminated with modern lighting that washed both the grounds to the front of the villa and the villa itself in a series of changing colours. In midwinter perhaps the effect might have been attractive, but now the bright illumination seemed at odds with the delicacy of the natural light that would ultimately fade, as Alena knew from her previous visits to St Petersburg, to a miraculously soft twilight.

With so many important people invited to the party they had to wait in the car for their turn to draw up alongside the red carpet and alight from their transport. Somehow, without her managing to see how he had done it, it was Kiryl who stood at her side, his hand beneath her elbow as her partner, whilst Vasilii stood slightly behind them. Alena could feel her whole body trembling just because he was touching her. Trembling with longing for him, and not revulsion as it should have been.

At the top of the villa's flight of white marble steps it wasn't their host and hostess who waited to greet them but instead a major-domo, who took their coats and then called their names up to another official who was standing at the foot of a very grand return staircase at the back of the marble hall

It was only at the top of these stairs that they were finally greeted by their host—a very powerful man indeed. But it was obvious to Alena from the way in which he greeted them both that he thought very highly of Kiryl and Vasilii.

His new wife, although outstandingly beautiful, looked both slightly petulant and bored—until she saw Kiryl and Vasilii, when her eyes widened alluringly and she gave them both a sultry come-on smile.

The fierce stab of angry female antagonism at the sight of another woman smiling allur-ingly at 'her' man caused Alena to lift her hand to her heart, as though to still its fierce thudding. Now she was jealous of another woman smiling at Kiryl on top of everything else!

Watching Alena, Kiryl frowned. She looked so fragile, her face pale and set. He reached towards her, but Vasilii was saying something to her and she turned away to listen to her brother. Naturally she would prefer talking to Vasilii than to him, given the way she felt about him, Kiryl recognised. But he intended to make amends to her—to make things right for her. Or at least as right as he was able to make them…

CHAPTER TWELVE

I<small>T WAS</small> over three hours since they had first arrived at the party. Alena's head was aching from the volume of noise created by the huge number of guests talking to one another, the sound intensified by the marble floors and drowning out the music being played by a world-acclaimed string quartet.

Alena turned towards Kiryl, intending to ask him if he thought there was any chance of the pop singer being heard later on in the evening, when she gave her performance, but he was deep in conversation with one of the many businessmen who had came to talk to him during the course of the evening. Although he had acted the part of attentive fiancé to perfection, never once leaving her side, they had barely spoken to one another. The emotional gulf between them was so wide that Alena could barely swallow for the pain of the throat muscles she had locked against her misery.

Uniformed waiters and waitresses were circling amongst the guests, carrying plates of canapés—small blinis heaped with smoked salmon and caviar—that gleamed beneath the light of the many chandeliers.

The man talking to Kiryl had finally moved away.

'I'm just going to the ladies,' she told him, handing him her still half-full glass of champagne.

Kiryl watched her walk away She looked like a delicate lilac wraith, in a gown that was so much more elegant and restrained than the over-the-top outfits so many of the other female guests were wearing. The jewellery he had bought her after Vasilii had told him how irritated he was with himself for forgetting to get her mother's jewellery out of the London bank vault looked every bit as good on her as he had thought. He had seen the set in a store window and thought how much it would suit her, because of the purity of the diamonds and the elegant simplicity of its design. He had seen her touching the necklace every now and again during the course of the evening, but the look on her face when she had done so hadn't said that she was enjoying wearing his gift. Far from it, in fact.

A little to Alena's surprise, when she emerged from the ladies she found that Kiryl was standing watching the door, obviously waiting for her.

'I've just seen Vasilii,' he told her when she rejoined him. 'He's got some business matter he wants to discuss with someone he's met here, so he won't be travelling back with us.'

'Oh, I see.' That was all Alena could manage to say. It was ridiculous that the thought of the intimacy of journey home alone in the back of a chauffer-driven limousine with Kiryl should make her feel so weak with need.

'Alena....' Kiryl began, but Alena spoke at the same time, desperate to remind herself of the reality of their relationship.

'I haven't thanked you yet for this,' she told him, touching her new necklace. 'Vasilii said that you must have bought it for me to mark the success of your bid. I haven't congratulated you on that yet either. I meant to earlier, but...'

'I haven't accepted the contract. And the diamonds haven't got anything to do with it.'

Alena might have heard Kiryl's deliberately firmly spoken words, despite the backdrop of conversational noise all around them, but she still couldn't take them in. She looked up at him and then away from him, whilst her heart thudded and raced in confusion and disbelief, before managing to say, 'But you wanted it so much. It was what you wanted more than anything else. You said so. I heard you.'

'I know. I was wrong. Alena, I need to talk to you—properly. There's something I have to say to you about…about the future—your future. But not here. It's too noisy. Will you come back to St Petersburg with me?'

Alena nodded her head. Her heart was beating much more heavily now, as though it had recognised something ominous in Kiryl's words. She desperately wanted to know what he meant, but he was right—this was not the place to try and hold a private conversation.

Even when Kiryl had sent for their car, and they were installed in the back of it, he refused to say any more.

It was gone midnight when the car pulled up

outside the apartment block, but when Alena headed towards the entrance Kiryl caught hold of her hand and shook his head, saying, 'Let's walk. It will be easier for me to say what I know has to be said that way.'

Easier for him? What on earth could he have to say to her that would be hard for him to tell her?

'Very well,' she agreed.

Kiryl had released her hand now, and she missed the warmth of his touch. Without thinking about what she was doing, she moved closer to him—only to have him move away as he started to walk in the direction of the river, matching his pace to hers.

Here and there were a handful of pleasure boats on the Neva, and the lights from villas and parties being held on some of the islands were flickering in the distance. One of those islands was the one where they had stayed in winter. Why was she thinking about that now, when she knew how vulnerable she was to those memories?

'I intend to speak to Vasilii about this to-morrow,' Kiryl told her. 'But I want you to know now that since I have decided not to go ahead with the contract there is no longer any reason for us to marry. You don't need to worry, Alena. I shall make it clear to Vasilii that nothing we have shared will ever become known to anyone else. Vasilii can make it known publicly that *you* were the one to end our engagement. From the way in which men were looking at you tonight I know that I shall be much pitied for losing such a beautiful and charming bride-to-be.'

Beyond them the Neva gleamed silver-blue beneath the pale sky, but for once Alena was oblivious to its beauty.

'You have turned down the contract because you don't want to marry me?' Alena guessed.

Oh, the agony and the shame of knowing how bereft she felt. How humiliating it was to know that, against all good sense, a part of her heart had been clinging to the hope that somehow—miraculously—their marriage could bring them together.

Kiryl stopped walking to turn and look down into Alena's upturned face.

'I want to give you your freedom, Alena. Nothing I can do can make amends for the hurt and the damage I've caused you, but at least I can set you free from a marriage I know you don't want.'

'You turned down the contract for that…for me?' She couldn't believe that.

'I was angry when you said what you did in London. Angry with you and then angry with myself. I took that anger out on you. But after you'd gone I couldn't forget what you'd said—just as right from the first time I kissed you I couldn't ignore the effect you had on me, no matter how hard I tried to ignore and deny it. I told myself over and over again that you meant nothing to me, and that the only reason I wanted anything to do with you was because you would make it easier for me to reach my goal. But a man can only lie to himself for so long.

'You were right to accuse me of choosing the wrong path when I set out to prove that I could be more successful than my father, but wrong to say that I didn't have a heart. I did have a heart—until my father ripped it apart and threw the pieces after me into the gutter. I thought I'd left it behind me there. I told myself that I was glad to leave it there, because without it I could never be hurt again. Without it I would never have to think about the pain of seeing the hurt in my mother's eyes when she talked about my father. Without it I'd never again have to suffer the shame of my Romany blood or the bitterness of my father's rejection. There was no place in my life for a heart filled with human emotions. That's what I told myself and that's what I believed—until I met you. Somehow, without me being able to do anything about it, you scooped up those discarded pieces of my heart and with every touch you gave me, every kiss, every word and look of love, you pieced it back together and gave it back to me again. Not that I was grateful to you. I wasn't. In fact if I could I would have torn it out again if I'd been able to. I didn't want your love. And I certainly didn't want to love you back.'

If Kiryl had heard her indrawn breath of shaky disbelief as she listened to what he was saying he was giving no sign of it, Alena recognised. She wanted to speak but she couldn't. Her chest felt too tight, her emotions too overpowering for speech.

'I didn't deserve your love, Alena. I didn't value it and I didn't value you. Because deep down inside I didn't value myself. I was still my mother's child, no matter what I had achieved, and that meant that in my father's eyes I would never be good enough. It took you to show me—to teach me that being good enough meant turning my back on my father's beliefs and reaching out instead towards my mother's gifts to me. The gift of life, the gift of knowing that love matters more than anything else, and the gift of knowing what really is strength and what really is weakness. I thought the feelings I had for you that I couldn't control were a weakness, but now I know that loving you would have brought me true strength if I had realised in time how much strength comes from being loved and giving love in return. I can't turn back the clock, no matter how much I wish I could. I can't expect you to forgive me and I don't. I can't bring back to life the love I killed. But what I can do is set you free to find love with someone else—someone who will recognise as I did not until it was too late just how lucky they are. And I can also try to grow into the man you once thought I was. Tomorrow I shall speak to Vasilii and tell him.'

'No.'

Alena's short, staccato delivery of rejection of his plans had Kiryl frowning slightly as he looked at her.

'Alena, it's all right,' he told her gently. 'There is no need for you to fear that Vasilii will try to force you to marry me. I won't let that happen.'

'I'm not afraid of that. But I *am* afraid of spending the rest of my life without you, Kiryl. I couldn't bear that. I thought I could, but even when I thought that I couldn't possibly still love you I found out that I did. At the house in London, when you…when we… You were right.'

Alena looked out across the river, not brave enough to look directly at Kiryl as she made her admission. Her chest lifted as she breathed in, in an attempt to calm herself. She failed as she exhaled unsteadily.

'When you said that you could make me want you, you were right. I knew I did, but I hadn't realised quite how much, how desperately, until then, until you held me. I'd told myself that it was just the you I'd created inside my own head I wanted—not the real Kiryl.

I was wrong. I felt so ashamed of myself, so angry with myself, but it didn't matter how much I wished I didn't love you—I knew that I did. If you really love me too, and you're not just—Kiryl!'

Alena gasped breathlessly as instead of answering Kiryl simply took her in his arms rather fiercely and kissed her, with a passion that showed quite clearly exactly how he felt about her.

Of course one kiss wasn't enough. And since they weren't the only lovers out walking in the milky light no one paid any attention to them as they walked entwined in one another's arms, pausing to exchange loving looks and even more loving kisses every few steps, until Alena whispered tremulously, 'I love you so much, Kiryl. So very, very much. I want you to make love to me properly tonight. I want us to be together like we were before. Only this time it will be even more special. I thought I wanted you to be the man I had created inside my head, but now I know that that man was simply a pale shadow of the wonderful person you really are. Your mother would be so proud of you—and so am I. Take me back to your hotel with you.'

He went so still that for a moment Alena thought she'd made a horrible mistake and misunderstood him, that he didn't really love her after all. But then he moved his head, and in the half-light she could see the sheen of emotion in his eyes.

'I've got a better idea,' he told her, his voice husky and slightly raw.

'Where are we going?' Alena asked, when he reached for his mobile and gave instructions for them to be picked up by a limousine company.

His, 'Wait and see,' was accompanied by a tender smile that drew a responsive surge of happiness from her own heart.

Half an hour later, speechless with delight, Alena had no need to ask him where they were as they stood together outside the house where they had stayed earlier in the year.

'But we can't just walk in,' Alena told him.

'Oh, but we can,' Kiryl assured her. 'You see, I booked it for our honeymoon. I told myself that as it would be expected that we honeymoon somewhere it might as well be here, but of course it wasn't the convenience of this place being so close to St Petersburg that was really motivating me.'

'No?' Alena teased him as they waited for one of the servants to open the door. 'Then what *was* motivating you?'

'Ask me that question again when we're alone in our bedroom—unless you want to embarrass the staff,' Kiryl responded, laughing at the pink colour warming her face as the door opened to admit them.

The servants, like all well-trained staff, showed no surprise at their unscheduled arrival, earlier than planned and in their evening clothes, or at their lack of luggage. Alena was feeling so euphoric that she didn't really care what they thought. All that mattered to her now was Kiryl and their love—as she told him over and over again in the magical white night hours that followed in the privacy of the bedroom, where Kiryl showed her over and over again how very much he loved her.

For the first time he could experience the intimacy of her body wrapped around his own as he had longed to that very first time—flesh to flesh, without any barriers between them. As she held him and caressed him within her soft sweetness Kiryl knew that he had at last found everything he would ever need or want. A soft moan, a small movement of her body and the urgency that created within his own had him taking them both soaring to the heights, to fall through space and time together wrapped in one another's arms.

Finally, when she was unable to stifle a yawn, he drew her close to him so that she could nestle her head on his shoulder, and told her, 'This is the beginning of the journey we will share for the rest of our lives, my darling one—the only journey I shall ever want to make from now on.'

'Mmm,' Alena agreed sleepily. 'Although, given that we didn't take any precautions, it could be that we'll soon be sharing that journey with a third party.'

A child. His child. Their child. A child who would grow up knowing just how much it was loved by his father as well as its mother.

Kiryl drew Alena closer. 'I love you so much,' he told her, and knew that it was true.

EPILOGUE

So, ARE you now prepared to admit that I was right about this marriage being the right thing for you?' Vasilii teased as he stood at Alena's side in a receiving line for the wedding guests who were now queuing up to congratulate the newly married couple.

'You wanted me to marry Kiryl because of the family reputation and your business interests,' Alena reminded her half-brother, turning away from him to exchange a loving smile with Kiryl as he reached for her hand.

'No,' Vasilii told her. 'I wanted Kiryl to marry you because I knew how much you must love him to have given yourself to him.'

Alena stared at her brother.

'It's true,' Vasilii assured her quietly. 'My father left the responsibility for your happiness with me when he died, Alena. I could never ever have abdicated that responsibility.'

'But Kiryl told you that I meant nothing to him.'

'He told me that, yes. But let's just say that I wasn't totally convinced. I know my own sex, Alena, and everything I'd heard about Kiryl told me that he was an honourable man. I decided that, given time, the two of you might just find that you wanted to be together.'

'So everything has worked out perfectly, then?' Alena teased him.

'Fortunately, yes—no thanks to that irresponsible woman who left you un-chaperoned. She had better hope that her path never crosses mine, because if it does I shall have something to say to her.'

A hard note had entered her brother's voice, and Alena knew better than to argue with him. Besides, she had far more important and pleasurable things to do—like basking in the loving look her new husband was giving her, and feeling her toes curl up in her shoes at the thought of not just the night ahead but all the nights they would share in the future. The nights and the days, and the happiness of knowing how strong their love for one another was.

As though he knew what she was thinking, Kiryl mouthed to her, 'I love you—now and for always.'

'I love you too,' Alena whispered back.

* * * * *

LARGER-PRINT BOOKS!

◆ Harlequin *Presents*~

PASSION GUARANTEED SEDUCTION

GET 2 FREE LARGER-PRINT NOVELS PLUS 2 FREE GIFTS!

YES! Please send me 2 FREE LARGER-PRINT Harlequin Presents® novels and my 2 FREE gifts (gifts are worth about $10). After receiving them, if I don't wish to receive any more books, I can return the shipping statement marked "cancel." If I don't cancel, I will receive 6 brand-new novels every month and be billed just $4.80 per book in the U.S. or $5.49 per book in Canada. That's a saving of at least 13% off the cover price! It's quite a bargain! Shipping and handling is just 50¢ per book in the U.S. and 75¢ per book in Canada.* I understand that accepting the 2 free books and gifts places me under no obligation to buy anything. I can always return a shipment and cancel at any time. Even if I never buy another book, the two free books and gifts are mine to keep forever.

176/376 HDN FER2

Name	(PLEASE PRINT)	
Address		Apt. #
City	State/Prov.	Zip/Postal Code

Signature (if under 18, a parent or guardian must sign)

Mail to the **Reader Service:**
IN U.S.A.: P.O. Box 1867, Buffalo, NY 14240-1867
IN CANADA: P.O. Box 609, Fort Erie, Ontario L2A 5X3

Not valid for current subscribers to Harlequin Presents Larger-Print books.

Are you a subscriber to Harlequin Presents books and want to receive the larger-print edition?
Call 1-800-873-8635 today or visit us at www.ReaderService.com.

HPLP11B